THE TIMELESS ODYSSEY

RANVIJAY SINGH DHAKA

Contents

Contents

FOREWORD

In the annals of human history, there are few narratives as captivating as the quest for knowledge and discovery. This story, a tapestry of courage, curiosity, and unrelenting pursuit, chronicles the remarkable adventures of five friends who dared to traverse the boundaries of time itself. From the ancient civilizations of the past to the enigmas of the future, their journey represents the very essence of human exploration and the quest to understand the unknown.

The tale begins with a groundbreaking invention—a time machine—that promises to unlock the mysteries of ages long past and those yet to come. Andrew, Thomas, Paul, Jacob, and Robert, each driven by a profound sense of curiosity and a shared passion for discovery, embark on a series of extraordinary adventures that span millennia. Their travels take them to the heart of the Mayan civilization, the grandeur of the Delhi Sultanate, and the zenith of the Vijayanagara Empire. They navigate the future and encounter the depths of historical enigmas, all while confronting the perils and wonders of each era.

Their journey is not without its challenges. From battles in ancient Delhi to the startling revelations of future worlds, they encounter the full spectrum of human experience. Yet, it is their unwavering commitment to their mission and to each other that defines their odyssey. The narrative delves into the triumphs and tribulations of their adventures, highlighting their resilience in the face of adversity and their deep bond as friends.

As their travels unfold, the story reveals profound insights into the nature of time, history, and human ambition. Their encounters with historical figures like Albert Einstein and the mystique of ancient civilizations offer a window into the complexities of science and culture. Each chapter of their journey weaves together the fabric of human experience, reflecting the timeless quest for knowledge and the enduring spirit of exploration.

However, their odyssey is not without its darker moments. The story poignantly captures the ultimate tragedy of their final journey, where the dreams of discovery give way to the harsh realities of fate. The loss of their comrades and the solitary survival of Thomas serve as a somber reminder of the inherent risks of their pursuit and the indomitable nature of the human spirit.

This tale is more than just an account of time-traveling adventures; it is a testament to the power of friendship, the quest for understanding, and the courage to face the unknown. It invites readers to reflect on the significance of their own journeys and the impact of their actions on the world around them.

In this narrative, we witness the profound impact of exploration on both the individual and the collective human experience. It is a celebration of the triumphs and trials that define our quest for knowledge, and a tribute to those who dare to dream beyond the confines of the present.

As you turn the pages, may you be inspired by the spirit of adventure that drives these five friends and find a deeper appreciation for the mysteries that lie beyond the horizon. Their story is a reminder that the pursuit of discovery is a journey that transcends time, and that the legacy of those who dare to explore endures long after their travels have ended.

PREFACE

In the realm of storytelling, few themes resonate as profoundly as the quest for knowledge and the boundless human curiosity that drives us to explore the unknown. The narrative you are about to embark on is a testament to this timeless pursuit, capturing the spirit of adventure and the desire to uncover the mysteries that lie hidden within the folds of time.

This story begins with an extraordinary premise: the invention of a time machine capable of traversing the ages. It is a concept that has fascinated minds for generations, inspiring both scientific inquiry and imaginative fiction. In this tale, the time machine becomes a vessel for an epic journey, taking its inventors—Andrew, Thomas, Paul, Jacob, and Robert—on an odyssey through the epochs of history and into the uncharted realms of the future.

Each chapter of their journey reveals a new facet of human civilization, from the grandeur of ancient Egypt to the enigmatic Nazca lines, and from the rich heritage of the Vijayanagara Empire to the distant reaches of the year 3450. Their adventures are marked by encounters with historical figures, the discovery of lost cultures, and the unraveling of age-old mysteries. The narrative explores the triumphs and tribulations of their quests, as well as the deep bonds forged through their shared experiences.

Yet, this story is not merely an account of time-traveling escapades. It delves into the very essence of what it means to explore and discover. Through their trials and triumphs, the friends grapple with profound questions about the nature of time, the impact of history, and the enduring spirit of human exploration. Their journey is as much about understanding the world as it is about understanding themselves.

As you read, you will witness the highs and lows of their adventures, from exhilarating discoveries to heart-wrenching losses. Their story serves as a reminder of the power of curiosity, the importance of friendship, and the courage required to face the unknown. It invites you to reflect on the significance of your own journey and the role you play in the ever-evolving tapestry of history.

This preface sets the stage for a narrative that is both grand in scope and intimate in its exploration of human experience. It is a journey through time that will inspire, challenge, and captivate. As you delve into the pages that follow, may you be transported to distant eras and distant futures, and may you find yourself inspired by the enduring quest for knowledge that drives us all.

Welcome to an adventure that transcends the boundaries of time, and to a story that celebrates the spirit of exploration and the quest for understanding.

Acknowledgements

This narrative is the culmination of countless hours of research, imagination, and dedication. I am deeply grateful to the individuals and sources that have significantly contributed to bringing this story to life.

Firstly, my heartfelt thanks go to Christopher Silvester for his insightful interview that provided invaluable perspectives on the intricacies of historical and speculative storytelling. His thoughtful questions and keen observations enriched the depth and authenticity of this narrative, allowing me to craft a story that is both engaging and intellectually stimulating.

I would also like to express my gratitude to Pearl S. Buck and her remarkable work, The Enemy. Her exploration of human conflict and resilience has been a source of inspiration and reflection throughout the writing process. Buck's portrayal of complex characters and challenging situations provided a framework through which I could examine the themes of courage, friendship, and the pursuit of knowledge within my own story.

Additionally, I extend my appreciation to the many historians, scientists, and storytellers whose works have laid the groundwork for the fictional time-travel adventures depicted here. Their contributions to our understanding of history and the human experience have been instrumental in shaping the context of this tale.

To my family and friends, thank you for your unwavering support and encouragement. Your belief in this project has been a driving force behind its completion.

Lastly, to the readers who embark on this journey through time and imagination, your engagement and curiosity are what make the craft of storytelling so rewarding. I hope this story inspires you as much as the process of creating it has inspired me.

Thank you all for being part of this extraordinary adventure.

PROLOGUE

In a world where the boundaries of time are but whispers in the cosmic wind, five intrepid souls embarked on a journey that defied the limits of human understanding. Their names—Andrew, Thomas, Paul, Jacob, and Robert—would become synonymous with the most audacious exploration of history ever attempted. Fueled by a fascination with the unknown and armed with a time machine of unprecedented design, they set forth on an odyssey across millennia, navigating the vast expanse of the past and future.

The journey began with the discovery of a device capable of bending the very fabric of time—a contraption that promised not just the power to observe history but to become part of it. What began as a quest for knowledge soon evolved into a saga of adventure, courage, and unforeseen consequences. The time machine transported them from the grandeur of the Mayan civilization to the turbulence of the Delhi Sultanate, from the splendor of the Vijayanagara Empire to the enigmatic realms of the distant future. Each era brought its own challenges and revelations, shaping their destinies in ways they could never have anticipated.

Yet, their explorations were not without peril. The journey to the Bermuda Triangle ended in tragedy, with the loss of four cherished companions and the harrowing isolation of Thomas on a desolate island. The weight of their sacrifices and the burden of their discoveries would forever alter the course of their lives.

As they ventured through the ancient landscapes of Egypt, deciphered the secrets of the Nazca Lines, and uncovered the mysteries of Easter Island, their tales of bravery and discovery captivated the world. The publication of Andrew's groundbreaking reports heralded a new era of understanding, and their fame spread across continents. But the accolades were tempered by the trials they faced, including the theft of their time machine and the challenges of repairing it.

Through triumphs and tragedies, the friends' unwavering resolve to explore the mysteries of history remained their guiding star. Their final journey, marred by the catastrophic effects of the Bermuda Triangle, left an indelible mark on their legacy.

This prologue serves as a gateway to their extraordinary saga—a testament to the human spirit's insatiable curiosity and the quest for knowledge that transcends the boundaries of time. As you delve into their adventures, prepare to be transported to realms both familiar and fantastical, where the past and future intertwine in a dance of discovery and destiny.

CHARACTER PROFILES

Andrew Turner – The Visionary Scientist

Andrew Turner is a brilliant scientist with an insatiable curiosity for the mysteries of the universe. His academic background in quantum physics and theoretical research makes him a leading figure in the scientific community. Tall and lean, with a perpetual glint of curiosity in his deep blue eyes, Andrew exudes an air of intellectual intensity. His laboratory is a testament to his passion—filled with complex equations scrawled on whiteboards, state-of-the-art equipment, and a plethora of scientific journals.

Andrew's drive for discovery extends beyond conventional boundaries. His fascination with the fabric of time and space led him to develop the time machine—a culmination of years of theoretical work and experimentation. Despite his brilliant mind, Andrew is known for his humility and dedication to sharing knowledge, often spending hours explaining complex theories in accessible terms. His commitment to understanding the universe makes him the natural leader of the group.

Paul Richardson – The NASA Scientist

Paul Richardson is a distinguished physicist working at NASA, specializing in space-time research and advanced propulsion systems. With a meticulous demeanor and a sharp intellect, Paul brings a pragmatic approach to the group's adventures. His background in aerospace engineering and theoretical physics is instrumental in refining the time machine and overcoming technical challenges.

Paul is characterized by his precise and methodical nature. Standing at a moderate height with an athletic build, Paul's appearance reflects his disciplined lifestyle. His keen analytical skills and problem-solving abilities make him indispensable, particularly when the time machine faces technical malfunctions. Paul's dedication to scientific rigor is balanced by a deep sense of camaraderie and responsibility towards his friends and their shared mission.

Robert Evans – The Ingenious Engineer

Robert Evans is a skilled engineer whose expertise in mechanical and electrical engineering has been crucial in the development and maintenance of the time machine. With a background in designing complex systems and solving intricate mechanical problems, Robert's hands-on approach and inventive spirit are vital to the group's success.

Robert is a rugged individual with a strong, muscular build, often seen with grease-stained hands and a focused expression. His practical skills and ability to think on his feet are complemented by his unwavering determination to overcome technical hurdles. Robert's love for tinkering and problem-solving drives him to constantly seek improvements in their technology, making him a key player in their time-traveling endeavors.

Jacob Lewis – The Compassionate Doctor

Jacob Lewis is a compassionate and highly skilled doctor, whose medical expertise provides critical support during the group's travels. With a background in emergency medicine and a deep commitment to healing, Jacob is known for his calm demeanor and ability to handle high-pressure situations with grace.

Jacob is of average height, with a warm, approachable presence and an empathetic nature. His medical bag is always packed with essential supplies and advanced tools, ready for any health crisis that may arise. Jacob's dedication to his profession and his friends' well-being make him a trusted and invaluable member of the team, particularly in situations where quick thinking and medical intervention are needed.

Thomas Clarke – The Corporate Strategist

Thomas Clarke, the group's corporate strategist, brings a unique perspective to the team. With a background in business management and strategic planning, Thomas is responsible for handling logistical and operational aspects of their time-traveling adventures. His expertise in negotiation, risk management, and organizational strategy ensures that their missions are well-coordinated and executed smoothly.

Thomas is a tall, well-groomed individual with a professional demeanor. His analytical mind and strategic approach are essential in navigating complex situations and ensuring that the team's resources are effectively utilized. Despite his corporate background, Thomas has a deep appreciation for history and science, which fuels his commitment to the group's objectives. His ability to stay calm under pressure and his knack for problem-solving make him an essential part of the team.

I

The Idea

The Scientist's Routine

San Francisco, 1984. The city was a vibrant tapestry of innovation and tradition, with its iconic Golden Gate Bridge and bustling downtown contrasting sharply with the serene beauty of its coastal areas. Amid this dynamic cityscape, Andrew Turner, a scientist known for his groundbreaking work in quantum mechanics, toiled away in his laboratory. The office at The Science Association Bar California, though a hive of activity, often felt stiflingly mundane to Andrew. His routine, defined by meticulous experiments and theoretical calculations, had begun to feel like a monotonous cycle devoid of the excitement he once relished.

Andrew's apartment was a reflection of his solitary life. The walls were lined with shelves crammed with scientific journals, while abstract art offered a touch of color and inspiration. Despite the bustling city outside, his home was a sanctuary of quiet reflection. The view of the San Francisco Bay from his window was both soothing and isolating, a reminder of how distant he felt from the vibrant world he observed daily.

One crisp autumn morning, with the leaves turning golden and the air filled with a cool, invigorating breeze, Andrew's mood shifted. He felt an acute sense of ennui. The pursuit of theoretical physics seemed less compelling without the spark of exploration and camaraderie. On a whim, he decided to reach out to his old friends from university: Robert Evans, a talented engineer known for his unorthodox methods; Paul Richardson, a brilliant NASA scientist with a penchant for secrecy; Jacob Lewis, a dedicated medical doctor with a sharp mind; and Thomas Clarke, a well-connected professional at Robert Half International.

The South Park Cafe, nestled in a quaint corner of the city, provided the perfect setting for their reunion. The cafe's warm, inviting atmosphere, with its wooden tables and soft, ambient lighting, was a stark contrast to the clinical environment of Andrew's laboratory. As they settled in, their conversation naturally gravitated toward nostalgia, reminiscing about their youthful dreams and adventures.

Robert, with his usual exuberance, brought up their shared fascination with time travel. "Remember when we used to dream about traveling through time?" he said, his eyes gleaming with excitement. "Imagine the possibilities!"

Paul's eyes twinkled with a knowing glint. "Actually, you might not believe this, but NASA's been working on a time machine project. It's highly classified, but I could tell you a bit more."

The revelation was a jolt of energy for Andrew, who felt a surge of curiosity and excitement. The prospect of real-time travel rekindled a sense of wonder he hadn't felt in years. The friends agreed to explore this further, intrigued by the possibilities of adventure and discovery.

II

The Construction

The Blueprint

Paul's office in Seattle was a stark contrast to the bright vibrancy of San Francisco. It was a high-tech haven, filled with complex machinery, glowing screens, and piles of scientific papers. The walls were adorned with diagrams and blueprints of advanced technology. The atmosphere was charged with intellectual energy, and the air hummed with the promise of groundbreaking discoveries.

Paul unveiled the blueprint for the Temporal Displacement Apparatus with a flourish. The blueprint was a marvel of engineering, detailed and intricate. "This machine," Paul explained with a mix of pride and seriousness, "will use quantum entanglement to create a temporal wavefunction distortion. The Temporal Singularity Chamber will generate a localized singularity, allowing us to travel through time."

Andrew was fascinated. He poured over the blueprints, his mind racing with possibilities. Thomas, ever the pragmatist, focused on logistics and ensured they had the necessary resources. Robert's engineering skills were put to the test as he meticulously assembled the machine, his hands working with deft precision.

Jacob, though less involved in the technical aspects, played a crucial role in maintaining the team's morale. His calm demeanor and encouraging words provided a sense of stability amidst the whirlwind of activity. The team worked tirelessly, driven by a shared sense of purpose and the thrill of the unknown.

Months of intense effort culminated in the completion of the Temporal Displacement Apparatus. The day of the first test arrived on October 13, 1984. The machine stood before them, a gleaming testament to their hard work and dedication. The air was thick with anticipation as they prepared for the inaugural journey.

III

The First Journey

The Malfunction

With the machine set to transport them to ancient Egypt, the friends gathered with bated breath. The Temporal Displacement Apparatus, with its complex array of dials and gauges, was ready for its maiden voyage. Paul had meticulously set the coordinates, and the machine hummed with a soft, resonant energy.

However, just as the countdown began, a low battery warning flashed on the control panel. Paul, engrossed in a conversation with Andrew about potential future upgrades, failed to notice the critical warning. The atmosphere shifted from excitement to unease as the team scrambled to address the issue. They decided to have lunch to pass the time while the battery charged.

Unbeknownst to them, Robert, intrigued by the machine's complex mechanisms, approached it out of curiosity. Misinterpreting the control panel's settings and failing to fully understand Paul's instructions, he inadvertently inputted the date for 2000 BCE and activated the machine.

The Temporal Displacement Apparatus jolted violently. The room filled with a blinding flash of light, and the air crackled with energy. When the light dissipated, Robert was gone. Panic ensued as Andrew, Paul, Jacob, and Thomas realized that Robert had been transported to a distant future, 5984 AD.

Desperate to locate their friend, the group hastily set the machine's coordinates for Egypt. However, the machine, still unstable from the previous malfunction, malfunctioned again. Instead of arriving in ancient Egypt, they found themselves in 2000 BCE China, amidst the sprawling landscapes and primitive settlements of ancient civilization.

IV

Ancient China

The Encounter

The friends emerged from the machine into a world vastly different from their own. They stood amidst dense forests, rolling hills, and the majestic rivers of ancient China. The landscape was a pristine, untouched expanse, marked by the simplicity of early agricultural life.

The sight of villagers going about their daily routines was both fascinating and overwhelming. Farmers worked the fields with primitive tools, children played by the riverbanks, and artisans crafted their wares with skill and care. The harmony between the people and their environment was striking.

Their presence, however, did not go unnoticed. The friends' unusual attire and foreign demeanor aroused suspicion among the villagers. Soon, Chinese guards arrived, their stern expressions reflecting their concerns. The friends were apprehended and brought to the Grand Palace, an imposing structure that loomed over the landscape.

Inside the palace, they were subjected to a series of interrogations. Their attempts to communicate were met with confusion and distrust. The language barrier compounded their predicament, making it difficult to convey their intentions.

As the threat of execution loomed, the friends realized they had to act swiftly. Using their knowledge of the palace's layout, they navigated the labyrinthine corridors and evaded their captors. The escape was fraught with tension, their hearts racing as they slipped through the palace's hidden passages.

Finally, they reached the machine, concealed in a forest clearing. The friends, though exhausted, were determined to continue their journey. They set the coordinates for their next destination: Rome in 27 BCE, hoping that the advanced knowledge of their friend Robert could be found in the past.

V
Ancient Rome

The Grandeur of Rome

The Temporal Displacement Apparatus transported the friends to 27 BCE Rome, a city of unparalleled grandeur. The streets were alive with the clamor of merchants, the hustle of citizens, and the imposing architecture of ancient Rome. The city's splendor was a testament to its power and influence.

The friends marveled at the architectural masterpieces that surrounded them. The Colosseum, with its colossal structure and intricate design, stood as a symbol of Roman engineering prowess. The Forum, bustling with activity, was the heart of Roman political and social life.

Their encounter with Emperor Augustus was a stroke of fortune. Augustus, intrigued by their strange attire and curious tale, welcomed them to his palace. The opulence of the palace was overwhelming, with its lavish decorations, expansive gardens, and luxurious accommodations.

During their stay in Rome, the friends immersed themselves in the city's culture and history. They engaged with scholars and artisans, witnessing the creation of mosaics and the intricacies of Roman engineering. They explored the city's public spaces, attended forums, and marveled at the Roman baths.

Their time in Rome was a period of wonder and discovery. The friends were enchanted by the city's vibrancy and richness, finding a sense of fulfillment in their exploration of one of history's greatest civilizations.

VI
The Dystopian Future

The Robbery

Determined to find Robert, the friends set the machine to 5984, hoping to locate him in the future. However, their destination turned out to be 6956, a dystopian Seoul that starkly contrasted with the advanced future they had anticipated.

Seoul in 6956 was a grim spectacle of technological advancement marred by environmental decay. Towering skyscrapers loomed over a cityscape of pollution and neglect. The disparity between the affluent and the impoverished was glaring, with the wealthy living in opulent enclaves while the impoverished struggled to survive in the city's underbelly.

The friends' arrival was met with hostility. The locals, desperate and disillusioned, saw the friends as potential threats and robbed them of their resources. The friends were left stranded and vulnerable in the midst of the city's chaos.

Seeking refuge, they found an abandoned building on the outskirts of the city. The building was a relic of a bygone era, its walls crumbling and its interior strewn with debris. The bleakness of their surroundings was a stark reminder of the future's harsh realities.

Their experience in this dystopian future was marked by hardship and desperation. They faced the harsh elements, struggled to find food and water, and navigated the city's perilous landscape. The stark contrast between this future and the ancient civilizations they had previously visited was jarring.

VII
Tuvalu

A Serene Escape

Leaving the dystopian future behind, the friends set the machine to Tuvalu in 2020, seeking respite in a tranquil paradise. Tuvalu, with its pristine beaches and crystal-clear waters, was a stark contrast to the bleakness of Seoul.

Despite the challenges posed by the global pandemic, Tuvalu's isolation had preserved its natural beauty. The island's vibrant coral reefs and lush vegetation offered a serene escape. The friends reveled in the island's tranquility, snorkeling among the colorful marine life and participating in local cultural festivals.

The simplicity of life on the island provided a welcome reprieve from their tumultuous journey. They enjoyed the warm sun, gentle breezes, and the camaraderie of the island's residents. The friends found solace in the island's peaceful environment, reflecting on their adventures and the lessons learned along the way.

As they prepared to leave Tuvalu, they contemplated their journey and the experiences that had shaped their understanding of history and humanity. The island's beauty and serenity offered a moment of reflection and renewal before they faced the reality of their quest.

VIII
The Mayan Civilization

Arrival in the Heart of the Mayan World

The Temporal Displacement Apparatus hummed softly as the friends prepared for their next adventure. The machine's controls whirred to life, and with a flash of light, they were transported to the heart of the Mayan civilization in the year 750 CE.

As the light faded, the friends found themselves in a dense, tropical jungle. The air was thick with humidity, and the vibrant sounds of wildlife filled the atmosphere. Towering trees, adorned with lush greenery and colorful flowers, created a natural canopy that filtered the sunlight into a mosaic of dappled shadows on the forest floor.

Emerging from the jungle, the friends encountered a breathtaking view of a bustling Mayan city. The city was a marvel of ancient engineering, with towering pyramids, expansive plazas, and intricately carved temples. The grandeur of the Mayan civilization was on full display, with its advanced architecture and rich cultural tapestry.

Exploring the City

The cityscape was dominated by the Temple of Kukulcán, a majestic pyramid with steep, terraced sides and a towering pinnacle. The pyramid was adorned with elaborate carvings and frescoes depicting deities, mythical creatures, and celestial events. The friends marveled at the precision of the construction, which reflected the Mayans' advanced knowledge of mathematics and astronomy.

The central plaza was alive with activity. Priests, dressed in elaborate ceremonial attire, conducted rituals and ceremonies at the base of the temple. The scent of incense and the rhythmic beat of drums filled the air, creating a mesmerizing and immersive experience.

In the bustling marketplace, vendors sold a variety of goods, including vibrant textiles, intricately crafted pottery, and exotic spices. The marketplace was a vibrant hub of commerce and social interaction, where the friends observed the daily life of the Mayan people. The interactions between the vendors and customers were lively and animated, showcasing the rich social fabric of Mayan society.

Encounters with the Mayans

The friends' presence did not go unnoticed. Their unusual attire and advanced technology intrigued the Mayan people, who approached them with a mix of curiosity and caution. The friends struggled to communicate with the locals, relying on gestures and expressions to convey their intentions.

They were eventually brought to the city's ruler, a dignified and commanding figure who presided over the grand palace. The ruler, adorned with elaborate jewelry and a ceremonial headdress, was intrigued by the friends' appearance and their tale of travel from distant lands. The ruler's advisors and scholars gathered to hear their story, fascinated by the prospect of time travel and the wonders of future civilizations.

The friends were invited to participate in various ceremonies and cultural events, providing them with a deeper understanding of Mayan beliefs and practices. They observed the Mayan calendar, an intricate system of timekeeping based on astronomical observations, and learned about the significance of various celestial events.

The Mystery of the Calendar

One of the highlights of their visit was the opportunity to witness the Mayan Calendar in action. The Mayan calendar, a complex system of interlocking cycles, was used to track time and predict celestial events. The friends were fascinated by the precision of the calendar and the Mayans' ability to predict astronomical phenomena with remarkable accuracy.

They visited an observatory, a structure specifically designed for astronomical observations. From this vantage point, they observed the alignment of celestial bodies and the careful measurements taken by the Mayan astronomers. The friends were in awe of the Mayans' advanced understanding of the cosmos and their ability to integrate this knowledge into their daily lives.

A Cultural Exchange

During their stay, the friends engaged in cultural exchanges with the Mayan people. They participated in traditional dances, learned about Mayan mythology and religion, and sampled the local cuisine. The friends were struck by the Mayans' deep connection to their environment and their reverence for nature.

One memorable experience was attending a ballgame at the ball court, a sport that held great cultural significance for the Mayans. The game was a blend of athleticism and ritual, with players using a rubber ball and attempting to score points by passing the ball through a stone ring. The intensity of the game and the enthusiasm of the spectators provided a glimpse into the cultural importance of this ancient sport.

IX

The Delhi Sultanate

A Tumultuous Arrival

The friends had barely settled from their recent adventure when the Temporal Displacement Apparatus began to malfunction. The machine sputtered and whirred, and before they could react, a blinding flash of light engulfed them. When their surroundings finally came into focus, they found themselves in the heart of medieval Delhi, in the year 1310 CE.

The landscape was a stark contrast to the Mayan jungle they had left behind. The air was arid, with a hint of dust and the scent of burning incense. The city was bustling with activity, but there was an undercurrent of tension and unrest. The towering walls of the city fortress, adorned with battlements and watchtowers, loomed over the narrow, winding streets below.

As they emerged from their hiding place, the friends saw that they were in the midst of a tense period in the Delhi Sultanate. The grandeur of the city was marred by the signs of military presence and political strife. The streets were filled with soldiers clad in chainmail and armor, patrolling with a sense of urgency. The air was thick with whispers of rebellion and intrigue.

Meeting the Sultanate's Court

The friends soon found themselves in the midst of a political upheaval. They were apprehended by the Sultanate's guards, who, upon noticing their strange attire and advanced technology, suspected them of being spies. They were taken to the grand palace of Alauddin Khilji, a formidable and ambitious ruler known for his military conquests and ruthless governance.

The palace was a sprawling complex of courtyards, gardens, and opulent halls. The architecture was a blend of grandeur and austerity, reflecting the power and influence of the Sultanate. The friends were led into the presence of Alauddin Khilji himself, a figure of imposing presence with a sharp gaze and an air of authority.

The Sultan, intrigued by the friends' sudden appearance and their peculiar artifacts, demanded answers. The friends struggled to explain their situation, but their lack of understanding of the local language and customs made communication difficult. The Sultan, suspicious and wary, ordered their detention while he deliberated their fate.

Unraveling the Intrigue

As they were held in a dimly lit cell, the friends overheard fragments of conversation about a looming rebellion against the Sultanate. The city was rife with conspiracies, and there were rumors of a planned uprising by rival factions. The friends realized that they were caught in the middle of a dangerous political situation.

The situation grew more perilous as the day progressed. The friends learned that a rebellion was imminent, and the palace was on high alert. They had to find a way to escape, not only to save themselves but to avoid being entangled in the conflict that was about to erupt.

With their knowledge of future technology, the friends managed to devise a plan to escape from their cell. Using a combination of ingenuity and the limited resources available to them, they fashioned makeshift tools to unlock their cell and navigate through the labyrinthine passages of the palace.

The Rebellion Unfolds

Their escape coincided with the outbreak of the rebellion. The city erupted into chaos as rebels clashed with the Sultanate's forces. The friends found themselves in the midst of the conflict, with the palace under siege and the streets filled with the sounds of battle.

They navigated through the tumultuous streets, trying to avoid both the Sultanate's soldiers and the rebels. The friends witnessed firsthand the brutality of medieval warfare, with its intense combat and the impact of political power struggles on ordinary people.

The friends sought refuge in the bustling marketplace, which had become a chaotic battleground. The market, once a place of commerce and daily life, was now a scene of desperation and violence. The friends had to use their wits and courage to survive amidst the chaos.

A Fight for Survival

As the battle raged on, the friends were confronted by a group of armed rebels who mistook them for enemies of their cause. They were forced to defend themselves using whatever they could find, from makeshift weapons to the rudimentary techniques they had learned from observing the local fighters.

The skirmishes were intense, and the friends had to rely on their quick thinking and teamwork to fend off their attackers. Despite the odds, they managed to secure a temporary safe haven in an abandoned building on the outskirts of the city.

Their respite was short-lived, as the battle drew closer to their location. The friends knew they had to find a way to escape the city and return to their own time. They formulated a plan to reach the outskirts of the city, where they hoped to find a safer path to their Temporal Displacement Apparatus.

A Narrow Escape

As night fell, the chaos in the city began to subside. The friends took advantage of the darkness to make their way through the less guarded areas of the city. They navigated through the maze of streets and alleys, avoiding both rebel forces and Sultanate soldiers.

Their journey was fraught with danger, but they finally reached the location where their time machine had been inadvertently left behind. The machine had been damaged during their previous travels, and they had to make quick repairs to get it operational again.

With the machine repaired and their path cleared, the friends activated the Temporal Displacement Apparatus. The familiar hum and flash of light enveloped them once more, and they were whisked away from the tumultuous Delhi Sultanate.

Reflections and Departure

As they traveled back through time, the friends reflected on their harrowing experience in the Delhi Sultanate. They had witnessed the complexities of medieval politics, the brutality of warfare, and the resilience of people caught in the crossfire of power struggles.

Their journey had been a test of their courage and resourcefulness, and they emerged from the experience with a deeper understanding of history and the human condition. As they prepared for their next adventure, they carried with them the memories of their struggle for survival in a time of political upheaval.

The Temporal Displacement Apparatus hummed once again as they set off for their next destination, ready to face whatever challenges awaited them in their continued quest through time.

X

The Vijayanagara Empire

A Peaceful Arrival

After their harrowing experience in Delhi, the friends activated the Temporal Displacement Apparatus once more, eager to escape the turmoil and find solace in a more peaceful time. The machine whirred and hummed, enveloping them in a bright light. When the light faded, they found themselves in a different world: the flourishing Vijayanagara Empire during the reign of Emperor Krishnadevaraya, around the early 16th century.

The landscape before them was a serene contrast to the chaos of Delhi. The friends emerged into a vibrant and prosperous city surrounded by lush green fields and rolling hills. The air was filled with the fragrance of blooming flowers and the distant sound of melodious music. The city of Vijayanagara was at the height of its glory, a hub of culture, trade, and stability.

The architecture was majestic, with intricate temples and grand palaces showcasing the grandeur of the empire. The streets were wide and clean, lined with bustling markets and beautifully adorned buildings. The atmosphere was one of harmony and prosperity, a testament to the success of the Vijayanagara Empire.

Exploring the Empire

As the friends wandered through the city, they were struck by the vibrancy and vitality of the place. They marveled at the elaborate carvings and sculptures adorning the temples, depicting gods, goddesses, and mythical creatures. The temples were centers of not only spiritual life but also of learning and cultural exchange.

They visited the famed Hampi Bazaar, where merchants sold a variety of goods from silk and spices to precious stones and artifacts. The bazaar was a lively place, filled with the sounds of haggling, laughter, and the clinking of coins. The friends were welcomed warmly by the locals, who were intrigued by their foreign appearance but friendly and hospitable.

The city was also known for its impressive infrastructure, including well-planned irrigation systems and extensive water reservoirs. The friends took note of the advanced engineering and urban planning that contributed to the prosperity of the empire.

Meeting the Ruler

Their exploration eventually led them to the grand court of Emperor Krishnadevaraya. The emperor was renowned for his wisdom, justice, and patronage of the arts and culture. The friends were invited to the court as guests of honor, where they were greeted with great respect and curiosity.

The court was a grand spectacle of opulence and splendor. The emperor's palace was adorned with gold and precious stones, and the air was filled with the scent of exotic perfumes. The emperor himself was a regal figure, known for his benevolence and keen interest in the welfare of his people.

During their audience with the emperor, the friends were treated to a display of traditional music and dance, which showcased the rich cultural heritage of the Vijayanagara Empire. The performances were a blend of grace and skill, highlighting the artistic achievements of the time.

The emperor was fascinated by the friends' stories and their advanced knowledge. He shared insights into the governance and achievements of his empire, emphasizing the importance of unity, trade, and cultural patronage in maintaining peace and prosperity.

A Time of Unity and Prosperity

The friends spent several days in the Vijayanagara Empire, experiencing its peaceful and prosperous environment. They learned about the empire's efforts in promoting social harmony and economic growth. The emperor's administration focused on equitable distribution of resources and support for various art forms and intellectual pursuits.

They visited agricultural regions where advanced irrigation techniques were in use, ensuring bountiful harvests. The empire's commitment to infrastructure, education, and cultural development was evident in every aspect of life.

The friends also participated in local festivals and ceremonies, which celebrated the rich traditions and religious practices of the people. The festivals were vibrant and joyful, marked by colorful processions, elaborate rituals, and community feasts.

The unity and solidarity among the people were palpable. The society was characterized by mutual respect and cooperation, and the sense of community extended to every corner of the empire.

XI

The Year 3450

A Glimpse into the Future

The Temporal Displacement Apparatus hummed with anticipation as the friends prepared to travel into the far future. With a flash of light and a cascade of colors, they emerged in the year 3450, a time vastly different from any they had previously experienced. The world around them was a stunning amalgamation of advanced technology and futuristic landscapes.

The skyline was dominated by towering structures made of materials that seemed to shimmer and shift in the sunlight. The buildings were designed with organic curves and smooth surfaces, creating a skyline that resembled a blend of nature and technology. Floating vehicles glided silently through the air, their designs sleek and aerodynamic. The ground below was a mosaic of greenery and advanced infrastructure, seamlessly integrated into the urban environment.

The Cityscape

As the friends explored their surroundings, they marveled at the advancements that had shaped this future world. The city was an epitome of sustainability and innovation. Green spaces were abundant, with vertical gardens and hydroponic farms incorporated into the buildings. Renewable energy sources powered the city, and waste was efficiently recycled, creating a harmonious balance between technology and nature.

Smart surfaces and interactive displays were everywhere, providing real-time information and personalized experiences. People communicated using advanced holographic interfaces, and the concept of personal privacy had evolved into something more nuanced and sophisticated. The friends noticed that the population was diverse, with a blend of different cultures and backgrounds coexisting in this futuristic society.

Interactions with the Inhabitants

The friends were greeted by residents who were intrigued by their appearance and mannerisms. The inhabitants were friendly and eager to share insights about their world. They explained that the society had achieved a high level of technological and social advancement, with a focus on collaboration, equality, and environmental stewardship.

Education was highly advanced, with knowledge and skills being transmitted through immersive virtual experiences. The concept of physical schools had largely been replaced by virtual learning environments that allowed for personalized and interactive education. Medical technology had also progressed, with treatments and preventative care being delivered through nanotechnology and advanced genetics.

The Future of Society

The friends were introduced to a new way of living that emphasized well-being and balance. The society in 3450 had moved beyond traditional notions of work and leisure, embracing a more fluid and holistic approach to life. People engaged in activities that fostered creativity, personal growth, and community involvement.

Cultural and artistic expression thrived in this future world, with virtual and augmented reality playing a significant role in artistic endeavors. Museums and galleries showcased not only historical artifacts but also dynamic, interactive art forms that allowed viewers to experience art in new and immersive ways.

The concept of governance had evolved into a more participatory and decentralized model. Decision-making was driven by consensus and supported by advanced algorithms that ensured fair representation and effective policy-making. The emphasis was on creating a society that was inclusive and adaptable to the needs of its citizens.

A Journey of Discovery

During their time in the year 3450, the friends participated in various activities that showcased the advancements of the future world. They visited a cutting-edge research facility where scientists and engineers worked on projects related to space exploration, climate control, and artificial intelligence. The future was marked by a spirit of exploration and discovery, with humanity pushing the boundaries of knowledge and innovation.

They also attended a cultural festival that celebrated the diversity and creativity of the people. The festival featured performances, art installations, and interactive exhibits that highlighted the rich tapestry of human experience and imagination. The friends were struck by the sense of unity and celebration that permeated the event.

XII

Mongol Menace in the Year 3450

A Sudden Shift

The Temporal Displacement Apparatus activated with its usual hum, transporting the friends from the advanced society of 3450. However, a sudden malfunction jolted them out of their intended trajectory, thrusting them into an entirely different time and place. When the disorientation cleared, they found themselves amidst a scene of chaos and conflict.

The world around them had reverted to a historical epoch, but with a peculiar twist. Instead of a familiar ancient landscape, the friends were confronted with a dystopian vision of the Mongol Empire. This was not the time of Genghis Khan but a distorted future where Mongol influence had somehow persisted and evolved into a powerful and formidable force.

The Mongol Dominion

The Mongol Dominion of 3450 was a stark contrast to the advanced society they had just left. The landscape was a blend of rugged terrain and sprawling fortresses, reflecting the military prowess and strategic acumen of the Mongol rulers. Massive encampments and fortified cities dotted the landscape, with Mongol banners flying high above their strongholds.

The technology in this version of the Mongol Empire was a fusion of ancient tactics and futuristic innovations. Advanced weaponry and machinery were integrated with traditional Mongol warfare techniques. The Mongol soldiers, clad in a mix of armor and futuristic gear, commanded fearsome war machines that roared across the battlefield. The society was a blend of nomadic traditions and high-tech control, creating a unique and intimidating atmosphere.

Encounter with the Mongol Forces

The friends were initially mistaken for intruders and found themselves captured by Mongol patrols. The Mongol leaders, intrigued by these time travelers, decided to interrogate them. They were taken to a grand tent that served as the command center, adorned with a mix of traditional Mongol decor and futuristic technology.

The Mongol chieftain, a formidable figure named Khan Timur, demanded to know who the friends were and why they had appeared in their domain. The friends explained their situation, but the Khan, wary of potential threats, decided to keep them under close watch. They were placed in a secure enclosure, their movements monitored by advanced surveillance systems.

The Friends' Strategy

Realizing the precariousness of their situation, the friends devised a plan to escape and rectify the malfunction. They leveraged their knowledge of history and technology, attempting to blend in with the Mongol environment while secretly working on a solution. The friends used their understanding of Mongol tactics and technology to their advantage, creating a diversion to distract the guards.

They managed to access the temporal controls within their apparatus, making adjustments to correct the malfunction. However, their activities did not go unnoticed, and they soon found themselves facing Mongol forces determined to capture or eliminate them. The friends had to navigate a series of skirmishes and battles, using their ingenuity and resourcefulness to survive.

The Battle for Survival

The climax of their struggle came in the form of a massive confrontation between the Mongol forces and a rival faction that sought to overthrow Khan Timur's rule. The friends were caught in the crossfire, their survival depending on their ability to navigate the chaos and keep their temporal apparatus from falling into the wrong hands.

In the midst of the battle, the friends allied with a group of dissidents who opposed Khan Timur's dominance. Together, they fought against the Mongol forces, utilizing both advanced technology and strategic acumen to turn the tide of the conflict. The battle was fierce and tumultuous, with the friends playing a crucial role in tipping the scales.

A New Path Forward

After a grueling struggle, the friends managed to restore their apparatus to full functionality. They activated the device and, with a flash of temporal energy, escaped the clutches of the Mongol Dominion. As they departed, they looked back at the tumultuous scene, reflecting on the harsh realities of this distorted future.

With the apparatus now functioning correctly, the friends prepared for their next destination. They had faced an unexpected and daunting challenge, but their experiences had provided them with valuable insights into the resilience of different cultures and the impact of technological evolution.

XIII
The Critical Operation

A Tumultuous Time

The Temporal Displacement Apparatus whirred to life, shifting the friends from the chaotic Mongol landscape to the tumultuous backdrop of World War I. The year was 1917, and the world was embroiled in one of its most devastating conflicts. The friends emerged into the midst of a war-ravaged battlefield, with the sound of artillery and the sight of smoke-filled skies marking the desolation around them.

The friends quickly found themselves amidst a field hospital, where the horrors of war were starkly evident. Medical staff worked tirelessly, treating wounded soldiers who had been pulled from the front lines. The friends, accustomed to the advanced medical technologies of their own time, marveled at the rudimentary, yet earnest, methods employed by the doctors and nurses.

Jacob's Unexpected Role

Jacob, with his expertise in medicine, was immediately recognized as a valuable asset to the overwhelmed medical team. His skills and knowledge were quickly put to use, and he was thrust into a critical situation. A German soldier had been brought in with severe injuries—his condition was deteriorating rapidly, and the doctors were struggling to stabilize him.

Jacob, along with a team of dedicated doctors, took charge of the operation. As they worked to save the soldier's life, Jacob's focus was solely on the task at hand. The surgery was intense and fraught with complications, but Jacob's steady hands and sharp mind guided the team through the delicate procedure.

The Shocking Revelation

After hours of painstaking work, the surgery was deemed successful. The soldier, though unconscious, had been stabilized. Jacob and the other doctors, exhausted but relieved, awaited the soldier's recovery. It was then that they were informed of the soldier's identity—this critically injured man was none other than Adolf Hitler.

The revelation was both startling and disorienting. Jacob and the friends, aware of Hitler's future role in history, realized the gravity of the situation. The fact that they had just saved a man who would become one of the most notorious figures of the 20th century was both alarming and troubling.

Hitler's Gratitude

As Hitler regained consciousness, he was profoundly grateful to Jacob and the medical team for saving his life. His gratitude was genuine, and he expressed it with a fervor that left the friends uneasy. Hitler, intrigued by the strangers who had treated him with such skill, invited them to his quarters once he was well enough.

In his quarters, Hitler was cordial and curious, eager to learn more about his saviors. His gratitude took on a darker edge as he began to discuss his ambitions and plans. He revealed his grand vision for conquering the world, and to Jacob and the friends, it became clear that Hitler viewed them as potential allies in his quest for power.

A Dangerous Proposition

Hitler's offer to the friends was straightforward: he wanted their help in achieving his world-conquering ambitions. He was convinced that their advanced knowledge and skills could significantly bolster his plans. He spoke with a mix of charm and menace, trying to persuade them to join his cause.

The friends, however, were acutely aware of the future ramifications of Hitler's rise to power. They knew that aligning with him would have catastrophic consequences. They faced a difficult decision: whether to assist him and potentially alter history or to find a way to extricate themselves from this perilous situation.

The Secret Escape

Deciding that they could not risk the ramifications of aiding Hitler, the friends devised a plan to escape. They knew they needed to act quickly and discreetly. Utilizing their knowledge of the future and their understanding of historical contexts, they began to prepare for a covert departure.

Under the guise of continuing their assistance in the field hospital, they made their preparations. They subtly gathered the necessary tools and resources for their escape, all while maintaining their cover. Their departure had to be meticulously timed to avoid drawing attention from Hitler's guards or creating suspicion.

In the dead of night, with the chaos of the battlefield providing cover, the friends activated the Temporal Displacement Apparatus. They left behind the crumbling field hospital, the grateful yet ominous figure of Hitler, and the war-torn world they had briefly inhabited.

As they traveled through time, they reflected on the dangerous intersection of their journey with key historical figures. The gravity of their encounter with Hitler weighed heavily on them, but their escape marked a crucial step in their quest to navigate through time while safeguarding history.

XIV

A Journey to Bharatpur: Meeting King Surajmal

The time machine, an enigmatic device capable of bridging centuries and civilizations, had been in flawless operation until an unforeseen malfunction hurled Andrew, Thomas, Jacob, and Paul into an era they had not planned to visit. The landscape they emerged into was unfamiliar yet vibrant, the air thick with the scent of blooming flowers and the sounds of bustling life. The ornate architecture and the rhythmic sounds of traditional music signaled their arrival in the kingdom of Bharatpur, circa 18th century.

As the friends adjusted to their new surroundings, the grandeur of the Bharatpur fort became apparent. Its towering walls and intricate carvings spoke of a civilization rich in history and valor. Guided by a local resident who was both intrigued and honored to host such distinguished visitors, the friends made their way to the royal palace where they were to meet the renowned ruler, King Surajmal.

King Surajmal, a figure of regal bearing and commanding presence, welcomed the travelers with a mix of curiosity and hospitality. He was a man of wisdom and strength, his eyes reflecting the countless battles he had fought to protect his kingdom and the legacy of the Jat community he represented. The king, dressed in resplendent attire adorned with jewels and intricate embroidery, offered the visitors a seat in his opulent court.

As the friends settled into the rich cushions and listened to the harmonious blend of courtly music, King Surajmal began to recount the history and significance of the Jat community. His voice was a resonant blend of pride and reverence, each word carefully chosen to convey the depth of the Jats' heritage.

"The Jat community," King Surajmal began, "is one of the most distinguished and resilient groups in the history of our land. Originating as farmers and pastoralists, they have shown incredible adaptability and valor throughout history. The Jats have a tradition of fierce independence and a deep connection to the land they have cultivated and defended for centuries."

The king's words painted vivid images of the Jats' storied past. He spoke of their rise from modest beginnings to becoming a formidable force in the region. Their prowess in warfare, particularly their strategic acumen and their ability to mobilize quickly in times of conflict, had earned them a reputation as skilled warriors. The king detailed the Jats' role in various historical battles, including their resistance against invading forces and their efforts to secure and expand their territories.

"The legacy of the Jat community," Surajmal continued, "is marked by their strong sense of justice and their commitment to the welfare of their people. Their leaders, like the great Churaman Jat, established a legacy of governance based on principles of fairness and respect for their subjects. The spirit of the Jats is one of self-reliance and honor, and it is this spirit that has sustained us through countless trials."

Thomas, fascinated by the historical account, inquired about the specific challenges the Jat community had faced and how they had overcome them. Surajmal responded with a detailed recounting of the various struggles, from internal strife to external invasions, and the strategic maneuvers and alliances that had been crucial in navigating these challenges. The resilience of the Jat community, he emphasized, was not merely a matter of military might but also of deep-rooted cultural values and a shared vision of unity and progress.

Jacob, ever the historian, was eager to learn more about the cultural and social aspects of the Jat community. He asked about their traditions, festivals, and daily life. King Surajmal was pleased to share insights into the rich tapestry of Jat culture. He spoke of their vibrant festivals, such as the harvest celebrations, which were marked by joyous feasts, music, and dance. The Jats' social structure, characterized by a sense of community and mutual support, was also a central theme in the king's narrative.

Paul, with his scientific background, was intrigued by the agricultural advancements the Jats had implemented. King Surajmal explained how the community had utilized innovative farming techniques and water management strategies to enhance crop production and sustain their livelihoods. The king's admiration for the Jats' ingenuity and their ability to thrive in a challenging environment was evident in his detailed descriptions.

As the conversation progressed, the friends found themselves deeply moved by the king's account of the Jat community's history and values. The meeting with King Surajmal not only provided them with a richer understanding of the historical and cultural significance of the Jats but also offered them a profound appreciation for the enduring spirit of a people who had played a crucial role in shaping the history of the region.

After several hours of engaging dialogue, the friends expressed their gratitude to King Surajmal for the enlightening experience. The king, in turn, was pleased to have shared the legacy of the Jat community with such distinguished guests. As the time machine's malfunction had brought them unexpectedly to Bharatpur, the journey proved to be a serendipitous exploration of a remarkable chapter in history.

The friends bade farewell to King Surajmal and the kingdom of Bharatpur, their hearts and minds enriched by the encounter. As they prepared to return to their own time, they carried with them the stories and lessons of the Jat community—an enduring testament to the resilience and valor of a people whose legacy continued to inspire and captivate.

XV

Amazonian Shadows

A Lush and Mysterious World

The Temporal Displacement Apparatus hummed once more, transporting the friends from the tumultuous era of Great Surajmal to the dense and vibrant jungles of the Amazon Rainforest. The year was 2024, but their destination was an isolated region of the rainforest known for its breathtaking biodiversity and enigmatic beauty.

As they emerged from the apparatus, the friends were immediately enveloped by the rich, verdant landscape of the Amazon. Towering trees with broad canopies filtered the sunlight, casting dappled shadows on the forest floor. The air was thick with the earthy scent of foliage and the sounds of countless creatures—chirping birds, rustling leaves, and the occasional distant roar.

Despite the beauty, there was a palpable sense of tension. The rainforest, while enchanting, was also fraught with hidden dangers. The friends quickly set up camp, knowing that their journey had brought them to a region where the stakes were high.

A Dark Presence

It wasn't long before they discovered that their serene environment was marred by a more sinister presence. Reports from local sources and their own observations revealed that a network of drug dealers was operating in the area. These dealers, entrenched in illegal activities, were exploiting the Amazon's remote and inaccessible locations to cultivate and process narcotics.

The friends learned that the drug dealers had been using the rainforest's vast expanse to hide their operations, turning parts of the jungle into illicit plantations. The local communities, deeply affected by the drug trade, were caught in a cycle of violence and exploitation.

A High-Stakes Escape

Realizing the danger they were in, the friends knew they had to leave the area quickly. They decided to use their understanding of the forest's geography to their advantage. With the help of their advanced technology and survival skills, they navigated through the undergrowth, avoiding patrols and making their way back to their temporary camp.

As they prepared to leave the Amazon, they faced one last obstacle. The drug dealers, realizing that the friends had eluded them, launched a final search effort. The friends, using every trick they had learned, managed to stay one step ahead. They employed diversionary tactics and used their knowledge of the jungle to mislead their pursuers.

Finally, as night fell and the search efforts waned, the friends activated the Temporal Displacement Apparatus once more. With a mixture of relief and trepidation, they left behind the treacherous rainforest and its dangers, emerging into a new time and place.

XVI
The Heart of Africa

Arrival in the Savannah

The Temporal Displacement Apparatus whirred to life once again, transporting the friends from the Amazon Rainforest to the vast savannahs of Africa. It was the year 2100, a time of both extraordinary technological advancements and continued struggles for environmental and social justice. As they emerged from the apparatus, they were greeted by the sprawling plains of the Serengeti.

The landscape was a tapestry of golden grasslands stretching as far as the eye could see, dotted with acacia trees and occasional herds of wildebeest and elephants. The air was dry, filled with the earthy scent of dust and the distant sounds of wildlife. The friends set up their temporary base camp near a riverbank, where they could observe the diverse fauna and flora.

An Unexpected Encounter

Their peaceful observation was disrupted when they discovered evidence of illegal poaching activities in the area. Poachers had set up traps and were hunting endangered species, threatening the delicate balance of the ecosystem. The friends were appalled and decided to intervene.

They embarked on a mission to expose the poachers, gathering evidence and working with local conservationists who were trying to protect the wildlife. Their efforts led to a series of tense confrontations. The poachers were armed and dangerous, and the friends had to use both their knowledge of the terrain and their advanced technology to outmaneuver them.

A Legacy of Conservation

In the end, the friends managed to assist the conservationists in apprehending the poachers and dismantling their operation. Their actions contributed to the protection of endangered species and the preservation of the Serengeti's natural beauty. They left Africa with a sense of accomplishment, knowing they had made a difference in the fight against environmental exploitation.

XVII
A Meeting of Minds

A Serendipitous Encounter

In the year 1925, amidst the bustling academic atmosphere of Zurich, Switzerland, the Temporal Displacement Apparatus deposited Paul and his friends at a small but prestigious café known for its intellectual patrons. Their arrival was met with an inviting aura of curiosity and discovery. It wasn't long before they spotted the figure they were hoping to meet: Albert Einstein himself, engrossed in a deep conversation with a fellow physicist.

The friends approached, and with a polite introduction, Paul found himself engaged in a conversation with Einstein. The renowned physicist welcomed them with a warm smile and a nod of recognition. The setting was perfect: the café's walls were lined with bookshelves, and the air was filled with the scent of coffee and the hum of scholarly discussion.

A Conversation Begins

Paul: "Professor Einstein, it's an honor to meet you. Your work has profoundly influenced our understanding of the universe."

Einstein: "Thank you, Paul. The universe is indeed a fascinating subject. What aspects of physics intrigue you the most?"

Paul: "I've been particularly interested in quantum physics and the implications it has on our understanding of reality. I'd love to hear your thoughts on how it intersects with your theory of relativity."

Einstein: "Ah, quantum physics—an intriguing and, at times, perplexing field. I have my reservations about it, as you might know. It challenges many classical ideas and introduces a level of probabilistic uncertainty that seems counterintuitive to the deterministic nature of relativity."

Quantum Physics and Determinism

Paul: "Exactly. Quantum mechanics introduces concepts like superposition and entanglement, which suggest that particles can exist in multiple states simultaneously and affect each other instantaneously across distances. How do you reconcile this with the deterministic framework of relativity?"

Einstein: "The core of my discomfort with quantum mechanics lies in its probabilistic nature. I've often said that 'God does not play dice with the universe.' The theory of relativity, in contrast, provides a deterministic view of spacetime. It describes the fabric of the universe with elegant precision, where the position and momentum of objects are governed by well-defined equations."

Paul: "That's a fascinating perspective. Yet, quantum mechanics seems to suggest that at the quantum level, uncertainty and probability are fundamental. How do you view the potential for a unified theory that reconciles these differences?"

Einstein: "The quest for such a theory is indeed compelling. A unified field theory aims to merge the forces of nature into a single framework. My attempts to develop this theory have yet to yield a conclusive result, but I believe that it might be possible to reconcile quantum mechanics with relativity by discovering a deeper, underlying structure of the universe."

Metaphysics and the Nature of Reality

Paul: "Speaking of deeper structures, I've been exploring metaphysical questions related to the nature of reality. Quantum mechanics and relativity both seem to imply that our intuitive notions of space, time, and causality might be more fluid than we once believed. What are your thoughts on the metaphysical implications of your work?"

Einstein: "Metaphysics indeed plays a role in our interpretation of physical theories. My theory of relativity fundamentally alters our understanding of space and time, showing that they are not separate entities but aspects of a unified continuum. It also introduces the concept that the fabric of spacetime is influenced by matter and energy."

Paul: "Exactly, and quantum mechanics extends this fluidity even further. Concepts like the 'many-worlds' interpretation suggest that every possible outcome of a quantum event occurs in a branching set of parallel universes. This challenges our classical notions of reality and existence."

Einstein: "The 'many-worlds' interpretation is indeed provocative. It suggests a multiverse where all possible outcomes are realized, which contrasts with the classical view of a single, objective reality. This idea raises questions about the nature of observation and measurement, and whether reality exists independently of our perceptions."

The Theory of Relativity and Quantum Mechanics

Paul: "In the context of the theory of relativity, how do you perceive the concept of spacetime in relation to quantum fields?"

Einstein: "The theory of relativity describes spacetime as a four-dimensional continuum that is curved by the presence of mass and energy. Quantum field theory, on the other hand, deals with fields that permeate spacetime and exhibit quantum properties. Integrating these concepts requires a deeper understanding of how quantum fields interact with the curvature of spacetime."

Paul: "Yes, and string theory is one such approach that attempts to unify these ideas. It posits that fundamental particles are not point-like but rather one-dimensional 'strings' vibrating at different frequencies. This theory provides a framework where both quantum mechanics and relativity can be incorporated."

Einstein: "String theory is an interesting candidate for a unified theory. It proposes additional dimensions beyond the familiar four, which might accommodate the forces and particles described by quantum mechanics and relativity. However, it remains a theoretical construct and requires experimental validation."

The Future of Physics

Paul: "Given the current advancements and your own groundbreaking work, what direction do you believe future physicists should pursue?"

Einstein: "I think the future of physics will involve exploring the fundamental principles that underlie both quantum mechanics and relativity. We must seek to understand the true nature of spacetime and the forces that govern it. This journey may involve new mathematical frameworks and experimental techniques that we have yet to develop."

Paul: "Indeed, and interdisciplinary approaches could provide valuable insights. Combining physics with insights from philosophy, computer science, and even biology might lead to new breakthroughs."

Einstein: "An interdisciplinary approach is certainly promising. The boundaries between different fields of science are becoming increasingly porous. By embracing diverse perspectives, we may uncover new dimensions of understanding that transcend traditional limitations."

Conclusion of the Discussion

As the conversation continued, Paul and Einstein delved into more intricate topics, discussing the philosophical implications of quantum mechanics, the role of consciousness in measurement, and the nature of reality itself. The discussion was both enlightening and inspiring, reflecting the depth and breadth of Einstein's intellectual curiosity.

As the café's evening light began to fade, the friends and Einstein exchanged farewells. The meeting had been a profound exchange of ideas, bridging the gap between classical and modern physics and exploring the frontiers of human knowledge. With a renewed sense of wonder and understanding, Paul and his friends prepared for their next adventure, eager to apply the insights they had gained from one of the greatest minds in history.

XVIII
The Wonders of Australia

Arrival in the Land Down Under

Their next destination was Australia, and the Temporal Displacement Apparatus transported them to the year 2500. This future Australia was a land of striking contrasts—an advanced society existing alongside pristine wilderness. The friends arrived in a vibrant coastal city known for its harmony with the natural world.

As they explored the city, they marveled at the integration of cutting-edge technology with environmental sustainability. Solar panels and wind turbines were seamlessly integrated into the urban landscape, and the city was surrounded by protected natural reserves.

The Great Barrier Reef

Driven by their curiosity, the friends ventured to the Great Barrier Reef, now more vibrant and resilient due to successful conservation efforts. The reef was a stunning mosaic of colors, with coral gardens teeming with marine life. They dove into the clear waters, experiencing firsthand the beauty of this underwater paradise.

However, they soon discovered that a new threat loomed—a group of eco-terrorists aiming to exploit the reef's resources for profit. These individuals were using advanced technology to disrupt the delicate balance of the reef's ecosystem.

A Battle Beneath the Waves

The friends, equipped with futuristic diving suits and technology, engaged in a high-stakes underwater battle with the eco-terrorists. They navigated through intricate coral formations and used their knowledge of marine biology to counteract the terrorists' destructive actions.

After a fierce struggle, the friends succeeded in neutralizing the threat and ensuring the reef's continued health. They were hailed as heroes by the local community, who recognized their crucial role in preserving one of Australia's greatest natural wonders.

XIX

Robert's Dilemma in the Distant Future

A Futuristic Metropolis

The city of Chicago in the year 5984 was a sprawling expanse of gleaming towers and advanced technology. The skyline was dominated by structures that defied traditional architecture, with buildings twisting into the sky like organic growths. Hovering vehicles zipped between skyscrapers, their trails of light weaving intricate patterns against the darkened sky. The city was both awe-inspiring and intimidating, a testament to millennia of human progress and ingenuity.

However, amidst this bustling metropolis, Robert found himself in an increasingly desperate situation. He was alone, having been separated from his friends due to a malfunction in the Temporal Displacement Apparatus. For weeks, he had roamed the city in search of a way to reconnect with them, but his efforts had proven fruitless. With no food, water, or access to any form of livelihood, his predicament was becoming dire.

Desperation in a Futuristic World

Robert's days were a struggle for survival. The advanced infrastructure of the city, with its automated systems and self-sustaining technology, was a stark contrast to his immediate needs. He wandered through abandoned streets and deserted high-tech facilities, trying to find sustenance and shelter. The city's advanced security systems had long since been deactivated, leaving the vast urban landscape eerily silent and empty.

His stomach growled with hunger, and his throat was parched from lack of water. The advanced vending machines that once dispensed food and drink had long since stopped functioning, and the energy fields that powered the city seemed to have dimmed. Robert's only option was to scavenge for whatever he could find, though his efforts were largely in vain. The city's advanced materials were not easily accessible, and traditional means of sustenance were nonexistent.

A Search for Answers

Robert began to explore the city's central hub, where he hoped to find some answers. The central hub was the heart of Chicago's technological operations, a place where the city's systems were monitored and controlled. As he entered the control center, he found it eerily quiet. The once-bustling room filled with holographic displays and data streams was now dim and deserted.

He approached the central console, hoping to find information about his friends or perhaps some means of communication. The interface was alien, with holographic controls and symbols he did not recognize. He struggled to understand the technology, but the language and commands were beyond his comprehension. Frustration mounted as he attempted to navigate the system, but his efforts were met with silence.

The Encounter

Just as hope seemed to be fading, Robert noticed a flicker of activity in the control center. A small, autonomous robot, designed to perform maintenance tasks, whirred to life and approached him. Its eyes, glowing with a soft blue light, scanned Robert with curiosity.

Robot: "Human detected. Query: Are you in need of assistance?"

Robert: "Yes! I'm stranded here. My friends and I were separated, and I'm trying to find a way to contact them. Can you help me?"

Robot: "Assistance protocol activated. Analyzing temporal displacement signals. Please provide relevant data."

Robert: "I don't have any specific data. We were traveling through time, and something went wrong with our device."

The robot processed the information and displayed a series of symbols on its holographic screen. Robert struggled to understand the data, but the robot's advanced algorithms were working to locate any temporal anomalies or traces of the device's signal.

A Glimmer of Hope

After what seemed like hours, the robot emitted a series of beeps and displayed a new set of coordinates on its screen. It seemed to indicate a location outside the city, where a malfunction in the temporal displacement apparatus might have caused a ripple.

Robot: "Temporal anomaly detected. Coordinates provided. Recommend immediate investigation."

Robert felt a surge of hope. He thanked the robot, which acknowledged his gratitude with a soft beep and returned to its maintenance duties. With renewed determination, Robert set out towards the coordinates.

The journey took him through the outskirts of the city, past derelict structures and into an area that appeared to be a forgotten part of Chicago. The advanced technology had given way to remnants of an earlier era, and the environment was less hostile than the city center.

A Ray of Salvation

At the coordinates, Robert found an old research facility, its exterior weathered by time but still standing. Inside, he discovered a hidden control room, where ancient technology from a bygone era was preserved. The equipment was outdated compared to the advanced systems of the city, but it was functional.

As he examined the equipment, he noticed a console with a familiar interface—a relic from earlier attempts at temporal travel. With a combination of intuition and desperation, Robert managed to activate the system. He began inputting data, hoping to establish a connection with his friends.

The console hummed to life, and Robert's heart raced as he initiated a distress signal. The system was primitive compared to the futuristic technology surrounding him, but it was his best hope. He sent a broadcast message, hoping it would reach his friends wherever they were.

A New Beginning

Days passed as Robert awaited a response. The solitude and deprivation had taken their toll, but he remained hopeful. Finally, his patience was rewarded when a faint signal crackled through the console. It was a message from his friends, who had managed to locate his position and were en route to retrieve him.

With renewed energy, Robert prepared for their arrival. He gathered any supplies he could find and made his way to the rendezvous point indicated by the signal. The waiting seemed endless, but the thought of reuniting with his friends kept him going.

When they finally arrived, it was a moment of immense relief and joy. The reunion was heartfelt, and Robert's friends were quick to provide him with food, water, and medical attention. They had managed to repair the Temporal Displacement Apparatus and were ready to continue their journey.

As they left the futuristic Chicago behind, Robert reflected on his harrowing experience. The city had been a marvel of human achievement, but it had also shown him the harsh reality of isolation and survival in a world that had moved far beyond his time.

With his friends by his side and the Temporal Displacement Apparatus back in working order, Robert was ready to face the next adventure, hopeful that the trials of the future had strengthened him for whatever lay ahead.

XX

Reunited Again!

A Distant Future

The Temporal Displacement Apparatus whirred and hummed as it stabilized, the familiar sensation of time travel washing over the four friends—Jacob, Paul, Anna, and Nadia. They had journeyed through countless eras and faced myriad challenges, but the urgency to find Robert in the year 5984 gave them a renewed sense of purpose.

The cityscape that greeted them was nothing like they had seen before. The towering skyscrapers of Chicago were more magnificent and intricate than any they had imagined, their shapes bending and spiraling in ways that defied conventional architecture. Hover vehicles darted through the air, and holographic advertisements floated effortlessly above the streets.

The Search Begins

After arriving in the heart of the futuristic metropolis, the friends began their search for Robert. They quickly realized that locating one person in such a vast, advanced city would be no easy task. They had only vague coordinates and a temporal signal from the malfunctioning apparatus, which had led them here.

"Let's start with the last known signal," Jacob suggested. "If we can find the source, we might find Robert."

Anna nodded, checking her advanced gadget, a futuristic device that could interface with the city's tech. "According to this, the signal was strongest around an old research facility on the outskirts of the city. Let's head there."

Navigating the Metropolis

As they made their way through the city, they marveled at the technological advancements. Automated systems managed traffic and infrastructure, and the air was filled with the hum of advanced machinery. Despite the city's grandeur, there was an underlying sense of abandonment in certain areas, with some buildings and systems showing signs of neglect.

"Can you believe this place?" Nadia said, looking around. "It's like stepping into a sci-fi novel."

Paul, ever the scholar, was fascinated by the advanced tech. "The level of advancement is astounding. I wonder how they managed such progress. It's like they've transcended our current understanding of physics."

As they approached the outskirts, they noticed a stark contrast to the city center. The advanced technology gave way to older, more decayed structures. It was here, among the remnants of the past, that they found the research facility Robert had discovered.

Finding the Research Facility

The facility was an old, weathered building with a faded sign indicating its former purpose. The entrance was partially obstructed by debris, and the once-imposing structure seemed forlorn and forgotten. The friends carefully made their way inside, their footsteps echoing in the dimly lit corridors.

Inside, they found the control room Robert had previously activated. The room was filled with outdated technology, but some of the equipment still hummed with residual energy. Paul immediately started examining the consoles, trying to understand their function.

Anna spotted a familiar figure huddled in a corner. "Look!" she exclaimed. "It's Robert!"

A Joyful Reunion

Robert, weak and disheveled from his weeks of isolation, looked up in surprise as his friends entered the room. Relief washed over his face, and he struggled to stand.

"Robert!" Jacob called out, rushing to his side. "We finally found you!"

Robert's eyes filled with tears of relief. "I can't believe it. I thought I'd never see you again."

The friends quickly attended to Robert's needs, offering him food, water, and medical care. They set up a temporary camp in the control room, where Robert shared his harrowing experiences.

Planning the Next Move

As the friends discussed their next steps, they decided it was crucial to learn more about the future and the changes that had occurred since their last visit. The advanced technology of 5984 presented both opportunities and challenges, and understanding it would be key to navigating their journey.

Paul took the lead. "We need to gather as much information as we can about this era. If we can understand how this society functions, we might uncover more about our own future and how to navigate it."

Jacob agreed. "Let's explore the city and see what resources we can find. We might even uncover more about the temporal anomalies that led us here."

Exploring the Future

The next few days were filled with exploration and discovery. The friends ventured into various parts of the city, learning about its advancements and uncovering hidden aspects of its technology. They discovered that while the city had advanced tremendously, it was also facing challenges related to resource management and technological maintenance.

Robert, now feeling stronger and more integrated with his friends' support, was instrumental in deciphering the city's technology and uncovering data that might help them understand the future's trajectory.

A New Understanding

As their time in 5984 came to a close, the friends felt a profound sense of accomplishment. They had reunited with Robert, navigated the complexities of a future world, and gained valuable insights into the progress and challenges faced by humanity.

Before departing, they reflected on their journey and the lessons learned. The futuristic Chicago had shown them the heights of human achievement and the enduring spirit of survival and ingenuity.

With renewed hope and understanding, the friends prepared to continue their temporal journey, ready to face whatever challenges awaited them next. As they activated the Temporal Displacement Apparatus, they looked back at the city one last time, grateful for the experiences and eager for the adventures that lay ahead.

XXI

An Ancient Encounter

A Malfunction in Time

The Temporal Displacement Apparatus hummed erratically, its lights flickering as the five friends—Andrew, Thomas, Paul, Jacob, and Robert—braced themselves for another jump through time. Their goal was simple: return home. But as the apparatus whirred to a stop, they found themselves in an era far removed from their expectations.

The landscape around them was dramatically different from anything they had seen before. The sky was a deep azure, with the sun blazing brightly in the sky, casting long shadows over a sprawling, arid plain. Towering mountains loomed in the distance, and the air was filled with the sounds of a world untouched by modernity.

Arrival in 5000 BCE

The friends quickly adjusted to their new surroundings. They realized they had landed in ancient India, around 5000 BCE, during the epic era of the Mahabharata. The lush, fertile land was dotted with ancient settlements and grand palaces, and the people wore elaborate garments, their attire reflecting the grandeur of their civilization.

As they ventured further, they were struck by the grandeur of the structures and the sophistication of the society. The majestic architecture and intricate artwork spoke of a culture rich in tradition and knowledge.

Meeting Duryodhana

After some exploration, the friends found themselves near a grand palace, its spires reaching towards the heavens. They were discreetly observing the royal court of the Kuru dynasty, and it wasn't long before they encountered Duryodhana, one of the central figures of the Mahabharata.

Duryodhana was a towering figure, exuding confidence and authority. His regal attire and commanding presence made it clear that he was a leader of great importance. The friends watched from a distance as he conversed with his courtiers, his demeanor both charismatic and imposing.

Thomas, always eager to understand historical figures, commented, "That's Duryodhana. I've read about his complex character and his role in the Mahabharata."

Paul nodded in agreement. "This is an incredible opportunity. We're witnessing history firsthand."

The Secret Listening

Their curiosity piqued, the friends decided to follow Duryodhana discreetly. They trailed him to a secluded area where they found him in deep conversation with his advisors. The air was thick with anticipation as they overheard discussions about the impending great war—the Kurukshetra War.

As night fell, they noticed a gathering in a nearby grove. Illuminated by the soft glow of lanterns, a serene figure emerged—Lord Krishna, the divine speaker of the Bhagavad Gita. He was surrounded by a small assembly, and the ambiance was charged with spiritual reverence.

The friends, hidden among the trees, listened intently as Krishna began to speak. His voice was calm and authoritative, carrying a profound sense of wisdom.

The Bhagavad Gita

Krishna's discourse began with a profound explanation of duty and righteousness. His teachings were timeless, addressing the nature of life, the self, and the universe. He spoke about the eternal soul (Atman) and its journey through various lives, emphasizing the importance of performing one's duty without attachment to the fruits of actions.

"Arjuna," Krishna began, "you are confused and bewildered, thinking of your duties in terms of personal gain or loss. Understand that the soul is eternal, and death is merely a transition. Perform your duty as a warrior, not for the sake of victory or defeat, but because it is your dharma."

Paul, enthralled, whispered, "This is extraordinary. We're witnessing the birth of one of the most significant spiritual texts in history."

Jacob listened intently, absorbing the philosophical depth of Krishna's teachings. "It's fascinating how these teachings address the core of human dilemmas—duty, righteousness, and the nature of existence."

Krishna continued, delving into the concepts of karma (action) and yoga (discipline). He explained that one's actions should be guided by wisdom and detachment, rather than selfish desires.

"The path of selfless action," Krishna said, "leads to liberation and harmony with the divine. When one acts with a sense of duty and devotion, without attachment to outcomes, one transcends the cycle of birth and rebirth."

Reflections and Departure

As the discourse continued, the friends found themselves deeply moved by the teachings. The Bhagavad Gita's profound insights into the nature of existence, duty, and spirituality resonated with them, providing a new perspective on their journey through time.

As the gathering dispersed, the friends knew it was time to leave. They had witnessed a crucial moment in human spiritual history and gained insights that would stay with them forever. They quietly made their way back to the Temporal Displacement Apparatus, reflecting on the encounter.

Andrew, his mind racing with thoughts, said, "That was an extraordinary experience. The Bhagavad Gita's teachings are incredibly profound and relevant, even to our modern lives."

Robert agreed, adding, "We've seen so much on this journey, but this moment—hearing Krishna speak—has been truly enlightening."

With a sense of fulfillment and a deeper understanding of the human quest for meaning, the friends activated the Temporal Displacement Apparatus once more. They were ready to continue their journey, enriched by the timeless wisdom they had just encountered.

As they left 5000 BCE behind, they carried with them the echoes of Krishna's teachings, their minds and hearts forever touched by the ancient wisdom of the Mahabharata.

XXII

Arrival in 1984 and a New Resolve

Reaching San Francisco, 1984

The Temporal Displacement Apparatus finally hummed to a halt, and the familiar sights of San Francisco in 1984 greeted the five friends. They stepped out into a vibrant cityscape, characterized by its iconic Golden Gate Bridge, bustling streets, and the unmistakable blend of 1980s culture and technology. The sun was setting, casting a warm golden hue over the city, and the atmosphere was filled with the sounds of lively street conversations and distant music.

With relief and gratitude, Andrew, Thomas, Paul, Jacob, and Robert took a moment to appreciate the familiarity of the present time. They marveled at how different their surroundings were compared to the ancient lands they had just left.

A Moment of Reflection

Gathering at a cozy café overlooking the San Francisco Bay, they found a quiet corner to reflect on their incredible journey. As they sipped on their coffee, the conversation turned to their experiences and the lessons they had learned.

Andrew broke the silence. "It's incredible to think about everything we've seen—each era, each moment. From the ancient Mayan civilization to the Mahabharata, it's been a journey through the very essence of human history."

Paul nodded in agreement. "And the future we glimpsed, the year 3450—it was a stark reminder of what we might become if we're not careful. The challenges we faced and the threats we encountered made it clear that our actions today have far-reaching consequences."

Jacob, ever the practical thinker, added, "The lessons we've learned are not just historical curiosities. They're warnings and guides for our own time. The state of the future we saw underscores the importance of taking action now."

Robert, who had endured the hardships of 5984 alone, looked at his friends with a sense of resolve. "We've been given a unique perspective on the past and the future. It's up to us to use this knowledge to make a difference."

A Deep Conversation

As the evening wore on, the conversation grew deeper. They discussed their experiences and the insights they had gained, weaving together the threads of their journey into a coherent narrative.

Thomas reflected on their encounter with Lord Krishna. "The teachings of the Bhagavad Gita were profound. They spoke of duty, righteousness, and the nature of existence. It's a message that transcends time and culture. It reminds us that our actions should be guided by higher principles, not just immediate concerns."

Paul, always intrigued by scientific and philosophical concepts, added, "The discussions we had with Albert Einstein about quantum physics and relativity, and the spiritual wisdom we gleaned from Krishna, both point towards a deeper understanding of reality. They show us that our actions, both in the physical and metaphysical realms, have significant consequences."

Andrew, reflecting on their experiences with historical figures and future scenarios, said, "Our journey has shown us that the course of history is shaped by the choices we make. The past is filled with lessons, and the future is a canvas waiting to be painted by our actions."

Jacob and Robert, having faced the challenges of the future and the ancient past, agreed on the urgency of their mission. "We've seen what happens when humanity neglects its responsibilities," Jacob said. "It's clear that we need to take action now to prevent the depletion and destruction we witnessed."

Deciding to Act

With a newfound sense of purpose, the friends decided to take concrete steps to address the challenges facing the Earth. They discussed various initiatives and strategies to combat environmental degradation, promote sustainable living, and foster global cooperation.

Paul suggested, "We should focus on raising awareness about the importance of environmental conservation. Education is key to inspiring people to take action."

Thomas added, "We can also support and advocate for policies that promote renewable energy and reduce carbon emissions. It's essential to work with governments and organizations to create effective solutions."

Andrew emphasized the need for grassroots movements. "Local communities play a crucial role in driving change. We should support initiatives that empower people to take action in their own neighborhoods and cities."

Jacob, with his experience in dealing with crises, proposed, "We should also develop contingency plans and strategies to address potential future challenges. Being prepared can make a significant difference."

Robert, having seen the future consequences of inaction, agreed. "We need to act swiftly and decisively. The stakes are high, and our actions today will determine the world future generations inherit."

A New Beginning

As the night drew to a close, the friends felt a renewed sense of purpose. They knew that their journey through time had given them invaluable insights and a unique perspective on the challenges facing humanity. With their shared resolve, they were ready to embark on a new mission—one that would involve not just their individual efforts but a collective movement to safeguard the future of the planet.

As they left the café and walked through the streets of San Francisco, they felt a deep sense of gratitude for the experiences that had shaped their vision. They knew that their journey had only just begun, and the real work of creating a better future was ahead of them.

With their hearts and minds aligned, Andrew, Thomas, Paul, Jacob, and Robert were determined to make a difference. Their adventure through time had given them a profound understanding of the interconnectedness of past, present, and future, and they were committed to using their knowledge to build a more sustainable and harmonious world.

As they looked out over the sparkling lights of the city, they felt a sense of hope and anticipation. The journey they had undertaken had come full circle, and now it was time to embark on a new chapter—one where their actions would shape the destiny of the Earth and ensure a brighter future for all.

XXIII

A New Mission

The NGO's Impact

Over the next two decades, Andrew, Thomas, Paul, Jacob, and Robert dedicated their lives to environmental conservation through their newly founded NGO, "Guardians of Earth." Their organization became a beacon of hope and action in a world increasingly aware of environmental issues. The NGO spearheaded numerous initiatives: reforestation projects, renewable energy adoption, pollution control, and educational campaigns on sustainable living. Their work garnered international recognition and support, leading to tangible improvements in ecological health and public awareness.

The friends' efforts were not without challenges, but their shared dedication and the lessons from their extraordinary journey kept them united and motivated. They became known figures in the environmental movement, giving talks, collaborating with governments, and inspiring millions to join the cause.

Jacob's New Vision

After twenty successful years, Jacob began to feel a sense of restlessness. He had always been fascinated by the mysteries of history and the possibilities that time travel presented. He proposed a bold idea to his friends: to refix the Temporal Displacement Apparatus and embark on new adventures, exploring historical mysteries and becoming renowned figures in the process.

Jacob's enthusiasm was met with mixed reactions. Andrew, Thomas, and Robert were content with their current achievements and wary of the risks associated with time travel. Paul, while intrigued, was concerned about the potential implications of altering history or being involved in dangerous situations.

They decided to discuss the proposal in detail. Jacob argued that their previous adventures had provided them with invaluable experiences and that exploring historical mysteries could lead to even greater insights and contributions to humanity's understanding of its past.

A Deep Conversation

They convened in their favorite café in San Francisco, the same place where they had discussed their future plans years earlier. The conversation was intense and reflective.

Andrew spoke first. "Jacob, I understand your desire for new adventures, but we've worked so hard to make a difference in the present. What if our actions in the past could unintentionally disrupt the progress we've made?"

Jacob responded, "I've thought about that. We can be careful and strategic, ensuring that we only observe and document, without intervening. Our goal would be to understand, not to alter."

Thomas, leaning forward, said, "There's also the risk of getting caught up in events that are beyond our control. Time travel is unpredictable, and the consequences of even small actions could be significant."

Paul added, "But the knowledge we could gain might be worth the risk. We have the opportunity to uncover historical truths and mysteries that could enrich our understanding of human civilization."

Robert, who had seen the future consequences of inaction, concluded, "We've always been a team that faced challenges together. If we approach this carefully and responsibly, we might be able to gain insights that could benefit humanity even further."

The friends discussed the proposal from every angle, weighing the potential benefits against the risks. After much deliberation, they reached a consensus. They agreed to embark on a new journey, but with a firm commitment to maintaining ethical standards and minimizing any potential impact on the course of history.

Refixing the Temporal Displacement Apparatus

With their decision made, the friends set to work on repairing and recalibrating the Temporal Displacement Apparatus. They utilized their combined expertise to ensure that the machine was in optimal condition and could safely transport them through time.

The process was meticulous and required significant effort. They revisited their previous modifications, enhanced the machine's safety protocols, and conducted rigorous tests to ensure its reliability. The project was both exciting and nostalgic, as it rekindled their sense of adventure and curiosity.

Preparing for the Journey

As the apparatus neared completion, the friends made final preparations for their journey. They reviewed their plan, outlining the historical mysteries they hoped to explore and the precautions they would take to avoid interference with the past. They packed equipment for research, documentation, and communication, ensuring they were ready for any situation.

The day arrived when the Temporal Displacement Apparatus was ready for its next journey. The friends gathered around the machine, their excitement palpable. They felt a mix of anticipation and apprehension as they prepared to embark on a new chapter of their extraordinary adventure.

Embarking on a New Chapter

With the machine fully operational, they activated the controls and set their sights on the historical mysteries they wished to uncover. As the Temporal Displacement Apparatus hummed to life, the friends braced themselves for the journey ahead.

Their first destination was set to a pivotal moment in history—a place where they could explore ancient enigmas and gain new insights into the human experience. They were ready to face the unknown and continue their quest for knowledge, armed with their experiences and a deep commitment to making a positive impact.

As the machine whirred and the familiar sensation of time travel enveloped them, the friends felt a surge of excitement and camaraderie.

They were about to step into the past once more, with a renewed sense of purpose and a shared goal of uncovering the mysteries that lay hidden in the annals of history.

Their journey through time had come full circle, and now, as they ventured into new historical realms, they were poised to make even greater discoveries and contributions to the understanding of human civilization. The adventures that awaited them promised to be as thrilling and enlightening as those they had already experienced, and the friends were eager to embrace the challenges and wonders of their new mission.

XXIV
Journey to the Cradle of Civilization

Departure and Arrival

As the Temporal Displacement Apparatus powered up, the familiar hum of the machine filled the air, and the friends braced themselves for their latest adventure. The controls were set to 2000 BCE, targeting the heart of ancient Egypt, where the Pyramids of Giza stood as monumental achievements of early human engineering and ambition.

The sensation of time travel was always disorienting, a whirl of colors and sounds that seemed to stretch and compress reality itself. When the machine finally came to a halt, the friends stepped out into the dry, sunlit landscape of ancient Egypt. They were greeted by the vast expanse of the desert, dotted with the colossal silhouettes of the Great Pyramids.

The friends marveled at the sight. The Pyramids of Giza loomed majestically against the backdrop of the clear blue sky, their limestone blocks glowing golden in the sunlight. The iconic structures were even more breathtaking up close, their scale and precision awe-inspiring.

Exploring the Giza Plateau

The friends set up their temporary base near the base of the Great Pyramid, meticulously noting their surroundings. The pyramids were even more impressive in their original state, with vibrant limestone casings that once covered the entire structure, making them shine brightly like gigantic beacons. They could see the intricate stonework and the precision with which the blocks were cut and aligned.

Andrew led the team in documenting their observations. He recorded detailed measurements and took numerous photographs, capturing every angle of the pyramids and their surroundings. The Pyramid of Khufu, the largest of the three, stood as a testament to ancient Egyptian engineering prowess. The sheer scale of the pyramid, with its 2.3 million blocks, was both humbling and exhilarating.

The friends ventured inside the Great Pyramid through the descending passageway. The air was cool and musty, a stark contrast to the sweltering heat outside. They navigated the narrow corridors, their torches casting flickering shadows on the walls. The Grand Gallery, with its corbelled ceiling, was a marvel of construction. The intricate layout of the burial chambers and passages reflected the Egyptians' advanced understanding of architectural principles and their religious beliefs.

In the Valley Temple and the Sphinx, they observed the ceremonial practices that accompanied the construction of the pyramids. The Sphinx, with its enigmatic smile, seemed to guard the ancient secrets of Egypt. Its immense scale and the detail of its lion's body and human head were remarkable, and the friends speculated about its origins and purpose.

Encountering the Ancient Egyptians

The team's interactions with the locals were both enlightening and challenging. The ancient Egyptians were initially wary of the strangers in their midst but soon came to accept them as curious visitors. They were fascinated by the advanced tools and clothing of the time travelers, though they kept their true origins a secret to avoid any complications.

The friends learned about the daily life of the Egyptians, observing their agricultural practices, crafts, and religious rituals. They watched as workers labored on the construction of the pyramids, hauling massive blocks of stone using ingenious methods involving sledges, rollers, and levers. The logistics of pyramid construction were more complex than they had imagined, with thousands of workers involved in a coordinated effort spanning years.

Mysteries and Discoveries

The friends were particularly intrigued by the astronomical alignments of the pyramids. The precision with which the pyramids were aligned with the cardinal points and key astronomical events demonstrated the Egyptians' sophisticated understanding of the cosmos. They recorded observations of the pyramids' alignment with the stars and the sun, noting how these alignments were likely integral to the religious and ceremonial aspects of pyramid construction.

They also delved into the symbolic and practical aspects of the pyramids. The intricate carvings and hieroglyphs within the pyramids and surrounding temples provided insights into ancient Egyptian beliefs about the afterlife, the gods, and the pharaohs' divine status. The friends documented the significance of these symbols and their role in the pyramid's purpose as a monumental tomb.

The team spent several weeks immersed in ancient Egyptian culture, their days filled with exploration and discovery. They meticulously documented their findings, capturing the grandeur and intricacy of the pyramids and the daily life of the people who built them. The journey was both exhausting and exhilarating, a testament to the incredible achievements of one of history's greatest civilizations.

Return to the Present

When the time came to return, the friends prepared to leave with a sense of fulfillment and awe. They activated the Temporal Displacement Apparatus and bid farewell to the ancient world. The journey back was as swift and disorienting as the departure, and soon they found themselves back in their own time.

Andrew's Groundbreaking Report

Upon their return, Andrew dedicated himself to compiling and analyzing the data collected during their adventure. His work was extensive, involving careful analysis of their observations, comparisons with modern understanding, and synthesis of new insights gained from their firsthand experience.

When Andrew's report was published, it was met with widespread acclaim. The detailed descriptions, photographs, and analyses provided a fresh and profound understanding of the Pyramids of Giza and ancient Egyptian civilization. Andrew's meticulous work captivated both scholars and the general public, making it a bestseller.

The report not only shed new light on the architectural and cultural significance of the pyramids but also inspired renewed interest in Egyptology. The book's success was a testament to the friends' dedication and the remarkable nature of their journey.

Legacy and Reflection

The journey to ancient Egypt had left an indelible mark on each of the friends. They had witnessed the grandeur of the pyramids, uncovered mysteries of an ancient civilization, and contributed to the understanding of human history. Their work with the NGO continued, but the exploration of Egypt added a new dimension to their legacy.

As they reflected on their experiences, the friends recognized the profound impact of their adventures. They had not only enriched their own lives but had also provided valuable insights to the world. Their journey through time had become more than just a quest for knowledge—it was a testament to the enduring human spirit of exploration and discovery.

XXV

The Enigma of the Nazca Lines

Departure to Peru

The Temporal Displacement Apparatus whirred into action once again, its controls set to a new destination: the arid plains of southern Peru, circa 500 CE. The friends were eager to unravel the mystery of the Nazca Lines—mysterious geoglyphs etched into the desert floor that had puzzled historians and archaeologists for centuries.

As the machine came to a stop, the friends emerged into the dry, dusty landscape of the Nazca Desert. The harsh sun beat down on them, but their excitement about the journey ahead kept their spirits high. The desert stretched out before them, vast and seemingly endless, with the Nazca Lines sprawled across its surface like an enormous, enigmatic canvas.

Exploring the Nazca Lines

The Nazca Lines were an extraordinary sight. From their vantage point, the friends could see the immense scale and intricate designs of the geoglyphs, including spiders, monkeys, birds, and geometric patterns. The lines, made by removing the reddish, iron-oxide-coated stones from the desert surface to reveal the lighter soil underneath, stretched for miles and formed intricate patterns that were best appreciated from above.

The friends took to the skies in a specially equipped glider, using a combination of ancient techniques and modern technology to get a bird's-eye view of the lines. From this vantage point, the full complexity and precision of the geoglyphs were revealed. The sheer size and scale of the drawings were breathtaking, and the friends marveled at the skill required to create such expansive designs with the rudimentary tools available to the Nazca people.

Andrew meticulously documented their observations. He noted the variations in the depth and width of the lines, as well as the way the different figures seemed to align with specific points on the horizon. The lines' straight paths and geometric patterns suggested a sophisticated understanding of mathematics and geometry.

Engaging with the Nazca Culture

The friends also made efforts to engage with the local Nazca people. Although they were careful to blend in and not reveal their true origins, they observed and participated in some of the daily activities of the Nazca civilization. They learned about the cultural and religious significance of the lines, as well as the various theories that the Nazca people themselves held about their purpose.

They discovered that the Nazca Lines were believed to have had astronomical and ceremonial functions. Some scholars suggested that the lines might have been used in rituals to honor deities or to mark celestial events. The friends also learned about the methods used to construct the lines, including the use of simple tools and the cooperation of large groups of people.

The team was struck by the sense of mystery and reverence surrounding the Nazca Lines. The local lore suggested that the lines were created to appease or communicate with gods and spirits, reflecting the deep spiritual and cultural beliefs of the Nazca people.

Scientific Theories and Discoveries

The friends explored various scientific theories regarding the purpose and construction of the Nazca Lines. They studied the alignment of the geoglyphs with celestial bodies, such as the solstices and equinoxes, and considered how the lines might have been used to mark these important astronomical events.

One prevailing theory was that the lines served as an astronomical calendar, marking important celestial events and guiding agricultural activities. Another theory posited that the lines were part of ritual pathways used in religious ceremonies. The friends discussed these theories in depth, considering how the evidence they gathered supported or refuted each hypothesis.

The friends also investigated the construction techniques used by the Nazca people. They observed how the lines were made by carefully removing the top layer of stones to expose the lighter soil beneath. The precision of the lines and the meticulous planning required to create them were impressive, reflecting a sophisticated understanding of geometry and spatial awareness.

Return and Andrew's Groundbreaking Report

After several weeks of exploration, the friends returned to their own time, filled with new insights and discoveries. Andrew, ever the diligent researcher, began working on his report, compiling the data they had collected and analyzing the significance of their findings.

The report that Andrew produced was comprehensive and groundbreaking. It included detailed descriptions of the Nazca Lines, analysis of their potential purposes, and comparisons with other ancient astronomical and ceremonial structures. The report also featured stunning photographs and diagrams, showcasing the beauty and complexity of the geoglyphs.

When Andrew's report was published, it received widespread acclaim from both the scientific community and the general public. The detailed exploration of the Nazca Lines and the insights into their construction and purpose captivated readers and scholars alike. The report not only shed light on one of the world's greatest archaeological mysteries but also elevated the friends to international fame.

Global Recognition and Impact

The success of Andrew's report catapulted the friends into the spotlight. They were hailed as pioneers in the field of historical exploration and their adventures became the subject of documentaries, lectures, and academic discussions. Their discoveries contributed significantly to the understanding of ancient civilizations and their monumental achievements.

The friends' work inspired a renewed interest in the Nazca Lines and other ancient geoglyphs around the world. Researchers and enthusiasts flocked to the Nazca Desert to see the lines for themselves and to learn from the groundbreaking research that the friends had conducted.

Their journey to the Nazca Lines had not only advanced the understanding of one of history's greatest mysteries but had also cemented their legacy as explorers and researchers. The adventure exemplified the spirit of discovery and the quest for knowledge that had driven them throughout their travels through time.

Reflection and Future Adventures

As they reflected on their journey, the friends were filled with a sense of accomplishment and wonder. They had ventured into the heart of an ancient mystery and emerged with new knowledge and insights that had captivated the world.

With their fame secure and their mission to uncover historical mysteries accomplished, the friends began to contemplate their next adventure. The excitement of exploration and the thrill of discovery continued to drive them, and they were eager to see where their time-traveling adventures would take them next.

Their journey to the Nazca Lines had been a testament to their dedication and curiosity, and it had opened new doors for future explorations. The friends remained committed to their quest for knowledge, ready to uncover more of history's hidden secrets and continue their remarkable journey through time.

XXVI
The Mysteries of Easter Island

Departure to Easter Island

The Temporal Displacement Apparatus hummed with a fresh surge of energy, and the friends gathered around as Andrew set the coordinates for their next adventure: Easter Island, circa 1200 CE. Known for its enigmatic Moai statues and isolated location in the southeastern Pacific Ocean, Easter Island, or Rapa Nui, was a place of profound mystery and intrigue.

As the machine came to a gentle stop, the friends emerged onto the lush, verdant island. The air was humid and fragrant with the scent of tropical flowers, and the expansive ocean stretched out in every direction. They were greeted by the sight of the Moai statues, standing solemnly on their stone platforms, or Ahu, overlooking the island.

Exploring the Moai Statues

The Moai statues were a breathtaking sight. Each statue, carved from volcanic tuff, was adorned with intricate features and stood in various states of completion. Some were partially buried, while others were standing tall, their eyes made of coral and their red topknots, or Pukao, made of scoria.

The friends marveled at the sheer scale and craftsmanship of the statues. Andrew, Paul, Jacob, and Thomas walked among the statues, studying their proportions, placements, and the elaborate carvings that adorned some of them. The statues varied in size, with the largest reaching up to 33 feet tall and weighing as much as 82 tons.

The group noted the alignment of the statues with significant points on the island, such as the solstices and equinoxes. The precision of the Moai's placement suggested an advanced understanding of astronomy and a sophisticated knowledge of their environment.

The Construction and Transport of the Moai

The construction and transport of the Moai statues had long been a subject of fascination and debate among historians. The friends conducted a series of experiments to understand the techniques used by the Rapa Nui people. They examined the quarries from which the statues were carved, such as Rano Raraku, and observed the remnants of the carving process.

They discovered that the Moai were carved from volcanic tuff using stone tools, and the shaping of the statues involved intricate techniques to achieve the desired forms. The friends also investigated the methods used to transport the statues from the quarry to their final locations. They found evidence that the statues were likely moved using a combination of wooden sledges, ropes, and a sophisticated system of levers and rollers.

Their research revealed that the Rapa Nui people had developed ingenious methods to move the statues over long distances. They used a system of ropes and manpower, with the statues being rocked back and forth to simulate a walking motion. This method, combined with careful planning and coordination, allowed the statues to be transported and erected with remarkable precision.

Cultural and Historical Insights

As they explored the island, the friends also delved into the cultural and historical context of the Moai. They learned that the statues were created to honor ancestors and prominent individuals. The statues were believed to embody the spiritual essence of the deceased, and their placement on Ahu platforms was a way of connecting the living with their ancestors.

The friends spoke with local historians and shamans, gaining insights into the spiritual significance of the Moai. They learned about the religious ceremonies and rituals associated with the statues, including the process of dedicating and activating the statues through ceremonial rites.

The Moai statues were also linked to the island's social and political structures. The friends discovered that the statues played a central role in the power dynamics of Rapa Nui society, with different clans competing to erect the most impressive statues to demonstrate their status and influence.

Environmental Challenges and Cultural Impacts

During their exploration, the friends became aware of the environmental challenges faced by the Rapa Nui people. The island's limited resources and deforestation had led to significant ecological changes, affecting the ability to maintain and transport the Moai statues.

The friends observed the impact of these environmental changes on the island's society and culture. They learned that the depletion of resources had led to conflicts and changes in the island's social structure, ultimately affecting the production and placement of the Moai statues.

Their research highlighted the complex interplay between environmental factors and cultural practices. The friends documented how the island's ecological challenges influenced the development of the Moai statues and the societal changes that occurred as a result.

Return and Andrew's Groundbreaking Report

After several weeks of immersive exploration, the friends returned to their own time, brimming with new knowledge and insights about Easter Island. Andrew once again took on the task of compiling their findings into a comprehensive report.

The report detailed the construction, transportation, and cultural significance of the Moai statues. It included extensive documentation of the techniques used by the Rapa Nui people, as well as insights into the environmental and social factors that influenced the creation of the statues.

Andrew's report was met with widespread acclaim. The detailed exploration of the Moai statues and their historical context captivated scholars, historians, and the general public. The report provided valuable insights into one of the world's most enduring mysteries and shed light on the achievements of the Rapa Nui people.

Global Recognition and Impact

The success of Andrew's report further solidified the friends' reputation as leading explorers and researchers. Their discoveries on Easter Island were celebrated worldwide, and their work contributed to a deeper understanding of Polynesian culture and history.

The friends' findings inspired renewed interest in Easter Island and the Moai statues. Researchers and enthusiasts from around the world flocked to the island to see the statues and learn from the groundbreaking research conducted by the friends.

Their journey to Easter Island had not only advanced the understanding of one of history's greatest mysteries but also highlighted the importance of preserving and studying cultural heritage. The adventure demonstrated the value of exploring ancient mysteries and the impact that thorough research and documentation could have on global knowledge.

Reflection and Future Adventures

As they reflected on their journey to Easter Island, the friends felt a deep sense of accomplishment. They had uncovered new insights into the creation and significance of the Moai statues and had contributed to a greater appreciation of Polynesian culture.

With their reputation solidified and their mission to explore historical mysteries accomplished, the friends began to think about their next adventure. The excitement of discovery and the pursuit of knowledge continued to drive them, and they were eager to see where their time-traveling explorations would take them next.

Their journey to Easter Island had been a testament to their curiosity and dedication, and it had opened new possibilities for future explorations. The friends were ready to embark on their next adventure, confident in their ability to uncover the secrets of history and continue their remarkable journey through time.

XXVII
The Heist of Time

The Glorious Award Ceremony

The excitement of the friends' latest discovery had not only made headlines around the world but also earned them a prestigious international award for their groundbreaking contributions to historical research. The ceremony was a grand affair, held in the opulent halls of a renowned convention center. Luminaries from various fields gathered to celebrate the achievements of Andrew, Thomas, Paul, Jacob, and Robert.

Dressed in elegant attire, the friends stood on stage, beaming with pride as they received their award. The crowd applauded their exceptional work, and the media covered the event extensively. The time machine, once a closely guarded secret, was now on public display as a testament to their incredible journey through time. The machine, a marvel of engineering and imagination, was showcased with pride, drawing admiration and curiosity from all who saw it.

The Night of the Heist

The celebratory atmosphere of the evening was abruptly shattered when, in the dead of night, the time machine and the Temporal Displacement Belt were stolen. The heist was executed with precision, leaving no immediate clues for the authorities to follow. The next morning, the security team discovered the theft, and panic ensued.

The news of the stolen time machine spread like wildfire. Headlines blared across newspapers and news channels: "Time Machine Stolen: International Treasure Vanishes." The friends were devastated by the loss. They had not only lost a significant scientific achievement but also faced the fear of their invention falling into the wrong hands.

The Investigation Begins

An intense investigation was launched. Law enforcement agencies, private investigators, and security experts were brought in to solve the case. Forensic teams scoured the scene for evidence, while detectives interviewed witnesses and reviewed security footage.

The investigation revealed that the thieves had used advanced techniques to bypass the security systems. They had expertly disabled cameras and alarms, leaving no trace of their entry. The lack of evidence made the case even more perplexing, and despite numerous leads, the investigation hit dead ends repeatedly.

As weeks turned into months, the friends became increasingly anxious. The stolen machine represented not only their hard work but also their ongoing quest to explore and understand history. The pressure to recover the machine and restore their work weighed heavily on them.

The Thief is Unmasked

After months of tireless investigation, a breakthrough finally emerged. A tip-off led the authorities to a known criminal syndicate with a history of high-profile thefts. Surveillance footage from nearby areas and forensic evidence pointed towards a key suspect. The suspect, a skilled thief with connections to the criminal underworld, was apprehended.

Interrogations revealed that the thief had been hired by a shadowy organization interested in exploiting the time machine for their own purposes. The organization, driven by motives of power and profit, sought to control and manipulate historical events for their gain.

With the thief in custody, the authorities recovered parts of the time machine. However, the device had suffered significant damage during the theft. Components were missing, and crucial systems were compromised, rendering the machine less efficient.

Paul's Restoration Efforts

Despite the damage, Paul took on the challenge of restoring and improving the time machine. His deep understanding of its mechanics and dedication to his work were put to the test. Paul meticulously analyzed the damage, reconstructed missing parts, and upgraded various components to enhance the machine's performance.

The restoration process was complex and time-consuming. Paul worked long hours, often with little rest, to ensure that the machine would be operational once again. He collaborated with other engineers and scientists to design and install new safety measures, preventing future thefts and ensuring the machine's reliability.

The friends supported Paul in every way they could, offering assistance and encouragement. Their determination to see the time machine operational again was unwavering. After several months of rigorous work, Paul successfully repaired and enhanced the time machine, restoring its functionality and improving its efficiency.

A New Era of Exploration

With the time machine restored, the friends were eager to resume their explorations. They held a press conference to address the public, sharing the story of the theft, the recovery efforts, and the enhancements made to the machine. The media coverage was extensive, and the friends' resilience and determination were widely praised.

The ordeal had strengthened their bond and reinforced their commitment to their mission. The time machine, now more secure and efficient, was ready for its next journey through history. The friends were determined to continue their quest for knowledge and exploration, armed with new insights and experiences.

Their story of overcoming adversity and restoring their invention became an inspiration to many. The international recognition they received for their achievements, combined with the successful recovery of the time machine, marked a new chapter in their journey.

The Road Ahead

The theft and subsequent recovery of the time machine had been a tumultuous experience, but it also highlighted the importance of their work and the potential dangers associated with their discoveries. The friends were more determined than ever to use their time machine responsibly and to continue unraveling the mysteries of history.

As they prepared for their next adventure, the friends reflected on their journey and the lessons learned. They had faced challenges and setbacks but had emerged stronger and more united. Their resolve to explore, understand, and preserve history remained unshaken, and they looked forward to the new discoveries and experiences that awaited them.

The time machine, now a symbol of their resilience and dedication, was ready for the next chapter of their extraordinary journey. The friends were excited to embark on new adventures, confident in their ability to overcome any obstacles that might arise and eager to continue their quest to explore the depths of history and uncover its secrets.

XXVIII

The Bermuda Triangle Catastrophe

The New Quest: The Bermuda Triangle

Driven by their insatiable curiosity and the desire to unravel one of history's greatest mysteries, the friends decided their next destination would be the Bermuda Triangle in the 14th century. This enigmatic region, known for its perplexing disappearances and unexplained phenomena, promised to reveal secrets that had eluded explorers for centuries.

The team was eager to delve into the heart of the Bermuda Triangle, a vast expanse of the Atlantic Ocean stretching between Miami, Bermuda, and Puerto Rico. Its reputation as a site of bizarre occurrences and inexplicable vanishing ships and aircraft made it an irresistible challenge. They hoped to uncover the truth behind the legends that had fueled countless theories and speculations.

The Journey Begins

With the time machine restored and the Temporal Displacement Belt recalibrated, the friends embarked on their journey. As the machine hummed to life, the familiar sensation of temporal displacement enveloped them. The colors of the present world blurred and faded, giving way to the unknown past.

The journey to the 14th century was smooth at first. The friends found themselves emerging from the time vortex into the heart of the Bermuda Triangle, amidst a sea that looked both familiar and alien. The lush, tropical landscape of the Bermuda Islands, untouched by modern civilization, spread before them.

Exploring the Island

The friends set up camp on one of the uncharted islands within the Bermuda Triangle. The island was dense with tropical vegetation, vibrant wildlife, and mysterious ruins that hinted at a forgotten civilization. The air was heavy with an eerie sense of anticipation as they began their investigation.

Thomas, Andrew, Robert, and Jacob were determined to explore the island's strange features. They discovered ancient artifacts and remnants of structures that suggested the presence of a long-lost society. These findings only deepened the mystery, as there were no records of such a civilization in any known historical accounts.

As the days passed, the team made significant discoveries. They encountered inexplicable phenomena—unusual electromagnetic disturbances, sudden weather changes, and peculiar navigational anomalies that defied logical explanations. Their equipment struggled to function properly, and the temporal displacement belt seemed increasingly unstable.

The Catastrophe Unfolds

On the fourth day of their exploration, the team experienced a series of harrowing incidents. The time machine began to malfunction sporadically, with strange fluctuations in power and erratic behavior. The equipment that had once been reliable now failed without warning, and the disturbances in the area grew more intense.

In the midst of their investigation, the time machine's systems began to degrade rapidly. The Temporal Displacement Belt, crucial for their safe return, showed signs of severe damage. The team tried to repair it, but the effects of the Bermuda Triangle's enigmatic forces proved overwhelming.

The situation deteriorated quickly. A sudden, violent storm engulfed the island, accompanied by fierce winds and torrential rain. Lightning crackled across the sky, and the electromagnetic interference intensified. The friends struggled to maintain control of the time machine and their surroundings.

Amidst the chaos, a catastrophic surge of energy struck the time machine. The Temporal Displacement Belt, already compromised by the Triangle's effects, was completely destroyed in a violent explosion. The machine's systems failed, and the once-secure time portal collapsed.

The Loss

In the ensuing chaos, Andrew, Robert, Paul, and Jacob were thrown into the tempestuous sea. The violent storm and the explosive force of the time machine's destruction left no chance for survival. The friends were lost to the raging waters, their lives tragically cut short.

Thomas, who had been securing equipment on the island during the crisis, witnessed the devastating events from a distance. As the storm raged on, he struggled to find shelter and safety. The destruction of the Temporal Displacement Belt left him stranded, with no means of returning to their own time.

Thomas's grief was profound. He was now alone on the desolate island, surrounded by the remnants of their expedition and the haunting silence of the aftermath. The loss of his friends was a crushing blow, and the isolation was a stark reminder of the perilous nature of their quest.

The Struggle for Survival

With the time machine destroyed and no way to contact the outside world, Thomas was left to fend for himself on the island. The survival of a single person in such a hostile environment was a daunting challenge. He had to navigate the treacherous terrain, find food and water, and protect himself from the unpredictable weather.

The island's strange phenomena continued to perplex him. The electromagnetic disturbances and weather anomalies persisted, making daily survival even more difficult. Thomas's efforts to salvage any useful equipment from the wreckage proved futile. The island was isolated, and the chances of rescue seemed slim.

Thomas's days were marked by a desperate struggle for survival and an overwhelming sense of loss. The memories of his friends and their shared adventures haunted him, providing both comfort and sorrow. Despite the hardships, he remained determined to honor their legacy by continuing to explore the mysteries of the Bermuda Triangle.

The Aftermath

As time passed, Thomas's plight became known to the outside world. Search and rescue missions were launched, but the Bermuda Triangle's treacherous conditions made it a formidable challenge. The mystery of the friends' disappearance added to the legend of the Bermuda Triangle, further fueling its enigmatic reputation.

Thomas's survival and eventual rescue became a story of resilience and determination. His return to civilization was met with a mix of relief and sorrow. The world learned of the tragedy that had befallen the team and the perilous nature of their explorations.

Andrew, Robert, Paul, and Jacob were remembered for their courage and contributions to the pursuit of knowledge. Their legacy lived on through their discoveries and the impact they had made on the world. Thomas carried their memory with him, vowing to continue their work and seek answers to the mysteries that had claimed their lives.

A Solemn Reflection

Thomas's journey through the Bermuda Triangle was a testament to the risks and rewards of exploring the unknown. The tragedy underscored the dangers of pushing the boundaries of human knowledge and the profound impact of loss on those who venture into the depths of history.

The time machine, once a symbol of exploration and discovery, became a cautionary tale of the perils inherent in tampering with time and the unknown. The friends' story served as a reminder of the sacrifices made in the pursuit of understanding and the enduring spirit of exploration.

Thomas's experience on the island and his eventual return marked a turning point in the quest for knowledge. The journey of Andrew, Robert, Paul, Jacob, and Thomas had left an indelible mark on history, and their legacy continued to inspire future generations to seek the truth and embrace the mysteries of the past.

The Final Odyssey

Thomas, the sole survivor of the ill-fated expedition to the Bermuda Triangle, faced a future forever marked by the profound loss of his friends. After being rescued from the desolate island, he returned to the world with a heavy heart and a spirit irrevocably changed by the events he had endured.

The world greeted Thomas's return with a mixture of relief and sorrow. The media hailed him as a hero for his resilience and survival, but he was haunted by the memory of Andrew, Robert, Paul, and Jacob, whose absence left an irreplaceable void in his life. The narrative of their final journey became a poignant reminder of the perils of exploration and the fragile nature of human endeavor.

In the years following his return, Thomas dedicated himself to preserving the legacy of his friends. He authored a detailed account of their adventures, including the harrowing events of the Bermuda Triangle. His writings not only documented their discoveries but also served as a tribute to their courage and unwavering pursuit of knowledge. The book, while filled with a sense of mourning, was also a celebration of their achievements and the spirit of exploration that defined their lives.

Thomas lived a life marked by solitude but also by a profound sense of purpose. He continued to contribute to the field of historical research and exploration, driven by a desire to honor his friends' memory. He engaged with the academic community, sharing insights from his experiences and advocating for the responsible exploration of the unknown. His lectures and publications became a source of inspiration for those who sought to understand the mysteries of the past while acknowledging the risks involved.

Despite his public role, Thomas found solace in quiet reflection and the simple beauty of nature. He often retreated to serene locations where he could be alone with his thoughts. These moments of solitude provided him with a measure of peace and allowed him to process the loss of his companions. He found comfort in the belief that their legacy lived on through their work and the impact they had made on the world.

As he grew older, Thomas remained deeply connected to the memories of his friends. He occasionally visited places associated with their adventures, each visit serving as a tribute to their shared experiences. The pain of their loss never fully receded, but he learned to live with it, finding meaning in the knowledge that their quest for discovery had been noble and transformative.

In his later years, Thomas received recognition for his contributions to historical research and exploration. Awards and honors were bestowed upon him, not just for his survival but for his dedication to continuing the work that had defined his friends' lives. He accepted these accolades with humility, viewing them as a testament to the collective efforts of the group rather than individual achievement.

Thomas's final years were marked by a sense of fulfillment and quiet reflection. He lived with the knowledge that, despite the tragedy that had befallen them, their journey had not been in vain. Their discoveries and the lessons learned from their experiences continued to resonate with those who sought to uncover the mysteries of the past.

As Thomas's life drew to a close, he looked back on his odyssey with a mixture of pride and melancholy. The legacy of his friends and their shared adventures became a part of his own story, woven into the fabric of his life. He faced the end with a sense of peace, knowing that their spirit of exploration and their pursuit of knowledge had left an enduring impact on the world.

In the quiet moments of his final days, Thomas found solace in the belief that their journey had transcended time and space, connecting them in ways that surpassed the boundaries of their mortal existence. Their story, marked by triumph and tragedy, would continue to inspire future generations to seek the truth and embrace the mysteries of the unknown.

Thomas Clarke: Alone

Thomas Clarke's braveheartedness shone brightly in the face of unimaginable adversity. Stranded alone on the desolate Bermuda island after the catastrophic failure of the time machine, he found himself in a dire situation that would have overwhelmed a lesser man. With Andrew, Robert, Paul, and Jacob lost to the brutal forces of the Bermuda Triangle, Thomas faced a profound sense of isolation and responsibility.

The island, once teeming with potential for exploration and discovery, had now become a harsh and unforgiving environment. The dense foliage, treacherous terrain, and unpredictable weather were obstacles that Thomas had to navigate with both physical endurance and mental resilience. Yet, his courage never faltered.

Each day, Thomas demonstrated remarkable resourcefulness. He fashioned tools from the island's natural resources, using his engineering background to create makeshift shelters and fire-starting equipment. His survival skills, honed from years of strategic planning and problem-solving, became crucial. He used his knowledge of the environment to find fresh water, edible plants, and safe paths through the island's wilderness.

Despite the loneliness and the constant threat of danger, Thomas's spirit remained unbroken. He meticulously documented his experiences, creating detailed logs and sketches of his surroundings, a testament to his unyielding determination to make sense of the tragedy and preserve the legacy of his lost friends. His bravery was not just in his physical actions but also in his mental fortitude—he held onto hope and a sense of purpose, driven by the belief that his friends' sacrifice should lead to a greater understanding of their plight.

Thomas's bravery extended to his interactions with potential threats. The island, known for its mysterious and often perilous reputation, occasionally presented dangers from wild animals or sudden weather changes. Thomas faced these challenges head-on, employing both caution and assertiveness to ensure his survival. His calm and composed demeanor in these situations reflected a deep-seated courage and a refusal to succumb to fear.

In moments of reflection, Thomas honored the memory of his friends by continuing their mission to uncover the mysteries of the world. His resolve to understand what had happened and to honor their shared dreams kept him moving forward. Thomas's bravery was ultimately defined by his resilience and his unwavering commitment to the legacy of the adventures they had shared. His actions on the island, driven by an indomitable spirit, became a powerful testament to his character and the profound strength that emerged in the face of overwhelming odds.

ENCOUNTERS THROUGH TIME

The journey of Andrew, Thomas, Paul, Jacob, and Robert was not merely a passage through the annals of history but a series of profound encounters with some of the most influential and enigmatic figures across time. Each meeting left a mark on their lives, shaping their perspectives and leaving indelible impressions on those they encountered.

In the ancient realms of the Mayan civilization, the friends met with the wise priests and scribes of the Maya. These learned individuals were both intrigued and cautious about the strange visitors. The Mayans, who revered time as sacred and cyclical, were initially bewildered by the travelers' knowledge of their future. Yet, their conversations revealed a deep mutual respect for knowledge and mystery. The Mayan priests, sensing a greater purpose behind the strangers' visit, felt a mix of awe and apprehension as they shared their understanding of cosmic cycles and celestial events.

Their tumultuous journey through the Delhi Sultanate brought them face-to-face with the formidable Alauddin Khilji and his court. The tension was palpable as the friends, caught in the crossfire of political strife, struggled to navigate the volatile environment. Khilji's suspicion and the fear of espionage led to intense confrontations, leaving the friends to rely on their wits and resourcefulness to survive. The encounter with Khilji was marked by a complex mix of respect and enmity, as he grappled with the inexplicable presence of the strangers and their apparent knowledge of the future.

In the Vijayanagara Empire, the friends experienced a stark contrast—a time of prosperity and peace. They were welcomed with hospitality by the empire's rulers, who saw them as esteemed guests rather than threats. The grandeur of the empire was mirrored by the warmth of its people, and the friends were deeply moved by the sense of unity and solidarity that prevailed. Their discussions with the Vijayanagara nobles revealed a shared vision for a harmonious world, highlighting the universality of human values across time.

The leap into the future brought them into the year 3450, where they encountered a society far beyond their imagination. The advanced technology and utopian vision of this future world left them awestruck. Their interactions with future scientists and visionaries opened new horizons of understanding, though the ethical dilemmas and existential questions they faced also presented challenges. The friends marveled at the progress while grappling with the implications for humanity's future.

The catastrophic encounter with the Bermuda Triangle, however, cast a long shadow over their adventures. The mysterious forces of the Triangle proved to be beyond their control, leading to the tragic loss of four friends. Their final moments were marked by a mix of despair and determination, as they struggled to comprehend the nature of the enigmatic forces that claimed them. Thomas, left stranded and isolated, faced a profound sense of loss and solitude.

Their return to the past, where they met historical figures like Surjamal, added a new layer of complexity to their journey. Surjamal, a lesser-known but significant figure, embodied the struggle between ambition and morality. His interactions with the friends were characterized by a deep curiosity about their origins and a sense of camaraderie, tempered by the constraints of his time. Surjamal's presence in their story highlighted the interconnectedness of human experience and the often-overlooked narratives that shape history.

In their explorations of the pyramids of Giza, the Nazca Lines, and Easter Island, the friends encountered a range of characters—from ancient builders and astronomers to indigenous guides and local historians. These encounters were marked by a profound sense of wonder and discovery, as well as moments of tension and misunderstanding. The friends' respect for the cultures they visited and their efforts to understand the significance of these mysteries reflected their dedication to the pursuit of knowledge.

The international acclaim that followed their revelations brought them into the spotlight, and their subsequent loss of the time machine added a dramatic twist to their legacy. The thief's capture and the machine's repair became a testament to the friends' resilience and ingenuity.

Ultimately, the story of Andrew, Thomas, Paul, Jacob, and Robert is one of exploration, discovery, and profound human connection. Their encounters with historical and future figures reveal the timeless nature of human curiosity and the shared quest for understanding. Each meeting, each moment of tension, and each revelation contributed to a tapestry of experiences that transcended the boundaries of time, leaving a lasting impact on both their lives and the world they sought to explore.